GRANDPA'S STORIES ABOUT INDIA

By

Ram M. Saxena

This book is a work of fiction. Places, events, and situations in this story are purely fictional. Any resemblance to actual persons, living or dead, is coincidental.

© 2002 by Ram M. Saxena. All rights reserved.

No part of this book may be reproduced, stored in a retrieval system, or transmitted by any means, electronic, mechanical, photocopying, recording, or otherwise, without written permission from the author.

ISBN: 1-4033-6511-3 (e-book)
ISBN: 1-4033-6512-1 (Paperback)

This book is printed on acid free paper.

1stBooks - rev. 12/05/02

DEDICATED
WITH LOVE

TO

MY WIFE, MONA

Ram M. Saxena

PREFACE

When I was a child, I had heard many stories from my mother. When I grew up and traveled to other places in India in connection with my personal and professional work, I heard many real and imagined stories from the people I met. I also heard some very good stories from my loving wife Dr. *Mona*. Almost all these stories were interesting and entertaining. However, I found that *some* of these stories were not only highly entertaining and exciting but they were also highly inspirational focusing on the desirable and healthy values of life, which are of immense significance in the present day World of social turbulence and turmoil. Since I have been a lover of literature in English, Hindi, and Urdu languages for almost half a century, I have been reading all the stories, which I have been able to lay my hands upon. When I started thinking and recollecting, I found that the abovementioned stories had not been recorded anywhere. I had a very keen wish to tell these stories to my two dearest grandsons Dave and *Krsna*. But right now they are too young; they are only 14 months and 26 months old, respectively. Since I am already about sixty years of age and further since I have not been keeping well for sometime now, it occurred to my mind that I may or may not be still alive and/or physically and mentally capable of telling these stories to *Dave* and *Krsna* by the time they are grown up enough to understand. Hence, I decided to record these stories on the computer of my son Sumeet.

I started my work at our vacation home in Flagstaff. As I proceeded with my work, my dear daughter – in – law Rupal (who is a Physician) told me that these stories were so good – entertaining, exciting, and inspirational - that even other children and grown ups could enjoy reading them and imbibe some good life values. *Rupal* also suggested that I should write some short stories myself impinging upon some of those other good life values which had not been covered by the abovementioned stories. When I returned to Phoenix, my dear daughter *Seema* (who is also a Physician) shared Rupal's view. That came as a rather strong motivation to me, which was further reinforced by the encouragement I received from my loving wife Dr. *Mona*.

Inspired, thus, I decided to record the good stories referred to above and write some myself. This is how **Grandpa's *Stories About India*** was conceived.

Since I was writing these short stories, to begin with, for my two grandsons who are both US Citizens by birth, and since I am now permanently settled here in the USA, I have written these stories in such a manner so that the American readers (and other readers outside India) have no difficulty in understanding references to people, places, and customs of India.

Grandpa's Stories About India contains *twenty-five* short stories. Of these, *eight* stories are based on my own personal experiences. Another *eight stories* are based on real events narrated to me by others. *My late mother Krishna Devi had narrated three stories to me.* And I have written the remaining six stories on the basis of my own imagination.

For me writing of these short stories has been a most rewarding and wonderful experience of my life. As I wrote the stories narrated to me by my late mother, I could not only hear her sweet voice in my mind but also feel the touch of her affectionate hand. When I wrote the stories based on true events narrated to me by my wife Dr. *Mona*, my mind went back to those days of 1965 when we were newly married and she had narrated these events to me with all excitement and love. As I wrote the stories based on my own personal experiences, I felt as if I was transcending down the memory lane and reliving those past moments of my life.

Grandpa's Stories About India is being placed before the readers in all humility. Personally I shall be most happy if some day some reader (or listener) finds some good value in them and feels inspired to imbibe it.

I am grateful to *Mona, Rupal*, and *Seema* for inspiring me to write this book. Words are insufficient to express my gratitude to my son *Sumeet* who edited the manuscript and did almost all the computer work. Starting with my late mother *Krishna Devi,* I am thankful to all those people who narrated the events on which some of these stories are based. Thanks are also due to *1st Books Library* for helping me in the publication of ***Grandpa's Stories About India.***

I would like to close this with a prayer:

We meditate on the adorable light of the supreme Creator of the Universe. May His light, which is in our minds, guide our intellect in the pursuit of the Truth.

Phoenix, AZ
July 29, 2002

Ram M. Saxena

TABLE OF CONTENTS

PREFACE v
THE TORTILLA UMBRELLA 1
THE NOTORIOUS ROBBER 3
THE DEAF AND DUMB GIRL 7
NAAN - É – SHEERAZI 13
THE FEROCIOUS HYENAS 17
THE WOOLEN FULL SLEEVE SWEATER 22
THE KIND-HEARTED WOODCUTTER 26
THE ROYAL HORSE 31
JATNI'S ADMONITION 35
GAJA GHALE 38
NO DISTRACTIONS, PLEASE 41
UNITED WE STAND 45
THE CHRISTMAS CAKE 53
TEARS OF LOVE 57
SPEAK THE TRUTH (?) 61
THE ICE CREAM MAN 66
THE HINDU TEMPLE 70
THE RICH MAN AND THE SHOES 74
BEING METHODICAL 78
LIFE AND CHALLENGE 87
ENCOUNTER WITH A HOLY SPIRIT 91
LALA 97
THEFT 101
ACCIDENT 105

Grandpa's Stories about India

THE TORTILLA UMBRELLA

NOTE: when I was a little child, my late mother narrated this to me.

Once upon a time, there lived a King in a small state in India. He was a very honest, religious, and kind person. His people were always happy with him. He had a wife. Like her husband, the Queen was also a very kind and generous person. Every day after cooking the meal for every member of the family the
Queen used to cook a few extra ROTIS (Tortillas). She used to give these in charity to an old beggar who used to come every day to her for the same. In return, the old beggar used to pray for the health wealth peace prosperity safety and security of the King, the Queen, their family and their kingdom. Like this many years passed and everybody lived happily.

However, there were some bad people also in the kingdom as happens everywhere. They were not happy with the king. They were always in search of an opportunity to find the king alone so that they could ambush him, kill him, and take the kingdom in their own hands. The king being a wise man used to be careful in this matter. His bodyguards always surrounded him. Moreover, the king himself was a brave and skilled warrior.

But in spite of all care, mishaps do occur in the life of all of us. And that happened with the king also.

Once it so happened that the king accompanied by his friends and bodyguards went for hunting as used to be the practice and fashion in those days with kings, rulers and rich members of the society. The bad people, who were always after the king, came to know this. Secretly they also followed the king and his party.

While chasing a lion in the forest, the king somehow got separated from others. In his enthusiasm to kill the lion the king went on and on, deeper and deeper in the forest Eventually he went very deep into the forest far far away from everybody else. It was also the end of the afternoon and beginning of the evening. So the daylight had also started diminishing.

Totally unaware of his isolation from others and secret entrapment by his enemies, the king kept riding on his horse. Suddenly, two men appeared in front of him with naked swords in their hands. The king stopped the horse. He looked to the right; there were two men brandishing their naked swords at him. The king turned his eyes to the left; there also there were two men with naked swords in their hands. A skilled warrior, the king quickly saw with the edges of his eyes that on his back also there were two men with naked swords ready to attack him.

Surrounded thus, the king could see that there was no escape for him. Being a brave man of great honor, he decided to fight the men all-alone. The fight started.

However, a very strange thing happened during the fight. The king had no difficulty in attacking his enemies with his sword. But whenever his enemies tried to attack him, from somewhere lots and lots of Rotis (Tortillas) came and formed such a thick umbrella over and around the king that the attacker could not see anything of the king. Rendered completely helpless thus the enemies could not harm the king in the least the king kept killing his enemies one by one. He killed all of them in no time. Then, he gave up the idea of hunting for the time being and decided to return to his forest camp.

When the king returned to the camp he found everybody greatly worried about him and only too happy with his safe arrival. Next day the lion was killed and everybody returned to the town.

The king called his trusted men and told them about the attack in the forest. The king ordered that other traitors should also be found out and put in the royal prison. The king, however, did not tell anyone about the Rotis (Tortillas).

Completing all this, the king decided to retire for rest. He went to his palace. His Queen was awaiting him. The king narrated the entire episode to the Queen. When the king told her that all alone he had killed eight enemies, the Queen praised the king and said that she was proud to be wife of such a brave man. When the king told her about the tortilla umbrella, she kept solemnly quiet.

Going to her prayer room, the Queen knelt in front of the idols and thanked the Gods for the heavenly blessing in the form of the tortilla umbrella.

Indeed, what goes around comes around. Hence, we should be kind to others.

Grandpa's Stories about India

THE NOTORIOUS ROBBER

NOTE: When I was a little child, this was narrated to me by my late mother

Long long ago there was a robber. Nobody knew his real name. And nobody could ever muster courage enough even to ask anyone what his name really was. Everybody used to call him Kalia Dakoo i.e. the Black Robber. This was so because he had a dark jet-black complexion. He was notorious throughout the land he lived in for his anger, cruelty, and greed.

Kalia used to rob people on the roads whenever he could get a chance. He used to forcibly enter the houses of people and rob them at night. Whenever there was a wedding, Kalia knew that there would be money, jewelry, and valuable goods around. So he used to select such occasions in particular for his notorious deeds. People had become so scared of him that many people used to go elsewhere to far away places secretly to perform marriages in their families. Since most people used to be of modest means, they used to perform the ceremonies in a quiet non-ostentatious manner lest Kalia comes to know about it and robs them of everything making even the performance of the marriage impossible without sufficient means.

Not that there was no one in the land to prevent Kalia from doing what he did. The King of the land had already instructed all his police personnel to catch Kalia dead or alive. The kind King loved his people. Therefore, he had also announced a big reward for catching Kalia alive. This was done to encourage people to give clue as soon as possible about Kalia's movements so that King's police force could chase and nab Kalia.

But Kalia was too clever and cruel. With the help of his gang members, he could always know in advance where the King's police force was in search of him. Last moment he used to change the place and time of his attack. Thus, it had become almost impossible for the police to catch him. Moreover, whenever Kalia learnt that somebody had leaked information on his movements to the police, he used to kill that person mercilessly and hang his body at a public place with the warning that this is how those shall be treated who betray him. This had spread such a terror all around that people used to feel greatly scared even to pronounce his name lest Kalia cracks his anger on them.

Kalia used to hide in a forest near the town. People used to feel enormous fear even in entering the forest. But sometimes they had to go to the forest to fetch wood or herbs or similar things. Then, people including merchants had to pass through the forest if and when they wanted to go to other towns. Thus, people had no choice but to go through the forest. And it was simply too good for Kalia to rob them of their valuable possessions in the forest.

People had become totally fed up with the robberies and cruelty of Kalia. They had also developed a hidden anger against the King. They had started thinking that the King was too weak to do anything in the matter. This had also encouraged some people secretly to plan a *coup* against the King.

The King was a wise and brave man. Through his own trusted men, the King had known of the distrust in the minds of some people. He had also known about the secret plotters against him. First the King got the rebels arrested and put them in his prison. Then he decided to put an end to the menace of Kalia, the notorious robber.

Where there is a will, there is a way. Luckily, the King got an excellent opportunity to fulfill his desire.

Actually it so happened that the only daughter of the Nagar Seth (the richest man of the town) was to be married. The marriage party was to come from a nearby town. The bridegroom was also the only son of the Nagar Seth of his town. Thus, it was common knowledge that at the time of the wedding there would be cash, jewelry, and valuables of unbelievable value on the wedding scene.

Kalia knew about the wedding through his gang-men. He hatched plans for a major robbery on the occasion. Kalia was too clever. He knew that enormous security arrangements should be made to prevent the robbery and to catch him and other gang members on the occasion. Hence, to encourage his fellows to perform fearlessly and mercilessly in this task, Kalia ordered that all the gang-men shall participate in the robbery and everybody shall be paid hundred percent more than what had been paid in the past. Greed is among the worst enemies of the mankind. All the gang members agreed to take part in the robbery and grab the booty.

The King was also not sitting silently. He had ordered most elaborate arrangements for safety and security on the occasion of such a prestigious wedding in the town. He had secretly mobilized all his forces including the secret police. The King had also promised to reward heavily those of his servants who would get injured or die in the attempt to catch Kalia.

The Wedding day arrived. The entire town was beautifully decorated. There were arrangements at so many places to provide entertainment and treat to the prestigious guests. Apparently, there were some policemen to guard the place of the Nagar Seth. However, the real arrangements were hidden from most people.

The marriage party from the other town arrived, stayed, and everything went smoothly as expected. After the big dinner all went to their places. Everybody thought that Kalia had got scared with the arrangements by the King and had dropped the plan to rob.

However, just after the midnight when the wedding ceremonies had been almost completed, Kalia attacked the house of the Nagar Seth with full force. There were his gang-men everywhere – inside the house, on the house top, among the guests, outside the house, in the street, and so on. There were only a few policemen to prevent the robbers. Hence, instead of doing anything, they humbly obeyed the robbers and sat in a corner. The robbers completed their robbery and then left with the booty.

It was only when the robbers on the backs of their horses had left the heart of the town that the security forces retaliated. The police had planned the snare so beautifully and in so many loops that at each loop, the robbers suffered heavy losses of men and material. Many policemen also sustained injuries and some also died.

But the plan to capture Kalia was so perfect that Kalia sustained serious Injuries in his legs, hands and chest. Last he got hurt in the head and fell unconscious on the ground. The police ignored most of the other robbers and formed a heavy and thick loop around Kalia. Seeing their leader thus surrounded, the robbers ran away as fast as they could. Kalia was captured.

Kalia was taken to the prison. His case was presented in the court. He was sentenced to death. A day was fixed for his hanging to death at a public place. The day and time of hanging arrived.

Just before being hanged, Kalia was asked if he had a last wish. Kalia said that he wanted to say something to his mother. His mother was summoned on the scene. She went near Kalia. Kalia said something in the ear of his mother. Then, violently he bit off the ear of his mother with his teeth. The mother started bleeding and crying in severe pain. The King asked Kalia why he had done this and what he had said to his mother.

Kalia had told his mother "When I was a little boy I used to steal things. You used to simply laugh at it and keep the things. That encouraged me to steal more. I also started beating people who came my way. Gradually I became what I am today. If you had punished and stopped me in the beginning itself, I would not have become a notorious robber. And I would not have been sentenced to death like this. You are responsible for my ruin. So I am punishing you".

True, bad behavior, which is punished, tends to cease and bad behavior, which is not punished, tends to be repeated and repeated with vehemence. It is the duty of parents to prevent children from walking on evil paths in life.

Grandpa's Stories about India

THE DEAF AND DUMB GIRL

NOTE: Based on a story narrated to me by my late mother when I was a little child.

Long long ago, there lived a man in a moderate town in India. He was not very rich, not even rich, but compared with others in the society, we can say that he was rather very well to do. He was a good, wise, and honest man. He had his own small business which he used to run mostly all by himself. He had a wife. She was a perfect match for him; she was also good, wise, and honest. The man and his wife used to respect and love each other.

In due course of time, they got a daughter. She was not too beautiful but certainly she was not ugly. Much better than an ordinary girl, she was very graceful. On the eleventh day after birth, learned wise men were invited to perform special prayers and find a name for her. Such used to be the custom in those days. Even now many people follow this tradition. So the wise men came and performed the special prayers.

Then it came to finding a name for the newly born girl. The wise men considered the day and time of her birth, her physical features and the then prevailing celestial position. After considering all these and discussing the matter among themselves, they said that the girl could be most appropriately called Purnima (Full Moon) also because she had been born on the Purnima (Full Moon) Day. Purnima Day is still considered to be very auspices among people of almost all faiths. The wise men also said that in all her life, Purnima Day - the day of her birth - shall be very auspices and lucky for the girl. The name was readily and happily accepted and adopted. Then there was a big feast for all the friends and family members followed by celebrations in the form of dancing and singing. The day was over then.

The time began to fly as it does when we are happy. But no one knows what destiny has in store for him or her.

Purnima had just completed two years of age when her mother fell seriously ill with some epidemic. In those times medical facilities used to be very simple and those too, rather rare. Most of the medical care used to be what is now called Black Magic or Witchcraft. Before anything substantial could be done, Purnima's mother passed away. The little child was left behind with her father.

Being a kind and loving man, Purnima's father tried to do his best to look after the child. But then the child was too little and needed the loving care of her mother. Moreover, her father had his own business where he had to spend long hours. He soon discovered that in an attempt to look after both, the child and the business, really speaking, he was not doing justice to either.

People in the neighborhood, in the community, friends, and family also advised Purnima's father to get married again. He did not like the idea of a second marriage. He had heard and observed that second marriage was never happy especially for those who had a child with the first wife because all said and done, the stepmother never accepted the child of the earlier wife. He expressed his doubts openly. His friends and well-wishers told him that such is not always the case and there are so many good people in the world. Moreover, they told him that since he had no choice, he could always take a chance. They also told him that even after the second marriage, he would still be there to take care of the child. With a rather heavy heart, having no other alternative, he married again.

As happens in most of the cases, the stepmother kept showing false affection for Purnima for a couple of days. Then she realized that she had already established herself in the house of her husband who had started trusting her. Purnima's father also observed that the stepmother was affectionate to the child; so feeling relaxed thus, he started focusing on his business – leaving the house rather early in the morning and coming late in the evening fully assured that all was well at home.

But in reality, all was not well at home. Whenever Purnima's father was present, her stepmother used to show false affection for her. But as soon as the father left, she used to become negligent; instead of looking after the child she used to enjoy herself and take rest leaving the child uncared for, hungry and crying.

After some time the stepmother became pregnant and in due course gave birth to twin daughters. This changed the entire situation.

Hitherto, the stepmother used to be only negligent towards Purnima but now that she had her own daughters, she started inflicting cruelty on her – the little child of about three years who could not even speak properly and clearly.

One day, late in the afternoon, Purnima was hungry and crying for something – food or milk. The stepmother became so irritated and angry out of her hatred and jealousy against Purnima that she pushed her away very violently. Being a little child, Purnima could not withstand the jolt. Her head collided against the wall several feet away and then she fell on the ground totally unconscious. The stepmother only ensured that she was still breathing; she did not bother to see or do anything beyond this.

After a few hours, Purnima's father returned home. When he saw Purnima sleeping, he asked his wife about what had happened. The clever and crafty woman told him that the girl was just playing around; she fell on the ground tired, and then slept. The father, however, was not totally convinced. He tried to examine the girl. He immediately became suspicious that perhaps something serious had happened which the woman was hiding out of her fear.

The father called the medical man. The medical man carefully examined the girl. He gave some medicines to the child. The child woke up. However, she did not speak anything. The medical man tried to talk to the child. But the child simply gave a blank look. When the stepmother came near the child, she got extremely scared and started crying.

The medical man was a very experienced and wise man. So was Purnima's father. They had no difficulty in understanding that the stepmother had treated the child badly. But they had no way to know the truth. The truth remained hidden behind the thick curtain of falsehood created by the stepmother.

Days passed but Purnima did not speak. Whenever someone tried to talk to her, she simply gave a blank look. Apparently she was fine. Now it was clear to all that due to the unfortunate accident, Purnima had become deaf and dumb having lost her speech and hearing ability.

In a way this proved to be better for the stepmother. Now she could inflict her cruelty on the little child without the fear of anyone knowing about it.

Besides the fact that the stepmother now had her own twin daughters and Purnima was the child of her husband's first wife, the stepmother had one very important reason to be jealous of Purnima out of which emotion, she not only hated Purnima but also inflicted cruelty on her and derived sadistic pleasure out of it.

The twin daughters of the stepmother were ugly looking, Perhaps, due to the ugly thoughts of their wicked mother. But Purnima had a very graceful face. And most importantly Purnima had very long liquid gold colored hairs falling even below her knees. Whenever the stepmother saw this, she used to feel mad. But Purnima's father loved it and he had sternly instructed his wife not to cut Purnima's long hairs. Though the stepmother was wicked and cruel, she used to be rather scared of her husband. She knew that the husband had become suspicious of her and, in any case, she was totally dependent on him for everything in life. So much against her wishes, she could not cut Purnima's hairs. However, she had forced Purnima to keep her hairs bound in a lump on her head.

Since Purnima was still a child, her stepmother used to give her a bath and comb and tie her hairs. Whenever the wicked woman did this, sadistically she used to drive a small pin in Purnima's head to torture her. To hide this, she used to tie Purnima's hairs in a lump on the top of her head. The child used to cry and cry but being so little and moreover being deaf and dumb, she could not do anything about it. The wicked woman kept doing this for quite sometime. The result was that not only Purnima became more and more sickly but she also developed a constant headache. The time continued to pass as it always does; days turned into weeks, months, and years.

Purnima grew into a graceful adolescent. The stepmother insisted that the girl must be married immediately because she wanted to get rid of her. The father also thought that this way, at least, Purnima shall be able to escape the hatred and humiliation from her stepmother – still he had no idea about the torture part.

He tried hard to find a suitable match for Purnima but had no success. Frustrated by this, he tried to find just any match that was available. But in this also he failed. No one was ready to marry his son to a deaf and dumb girl with a permanent headache and a stepmother. But no one in the entire world knows the ways and enormity of God's love and mercy.

Since Purnima had grown up, now she used to take a bath herself and wash her hairs on her own without the help of her stepmother. One day it so happened that the stepmother along with her twin daughters had gone out to meet someone in the community. The father too had gone out as usual to his workplace. Purnima was all-alone. She used to like this, being alone all by herself.

After taking a bath and washing her hairs, Purnima was standing on the balcony of her house to dry up her long hairs in the shinning Sun. Engrossed in her own thoughts, she did not notice that there was a young man just across the street in front of her house, sitting on the ground and very tenderly patting the leg of his horse and at the same time, looking at her. When Purnima noticed and looked at him, the young man tried to talk to her. But through her bodily gestures Purnima told the young man that she was deaf and dumb. Still the young man wanted to talk to her. Through her bodily gestures again Purnima, a person of dignity and self-esteem, told the young man that she was all alone in the house and so if he wanted to talk to her, he could come to her house later on. He was a wise and an honorable man. So he left. But before so doing, he made it clear to Purnima that he shall come again.

Next day was a holiday for Purnima's father. So he was at home. There came a knock on the door. When the stepmother opened the door, the same young man was there. She asked him what did he want. He told her that he wanted to talk to the eldest man in the family. She escorted him to her husband in the sitting room.

Meeting Purnima's father the young man offered his respects and then told him about himself, his family, and his own background. He said that he belonged to a respectable family, that he had just completed the first stage of his life *viz* studentship (in those days called as Brahmacharya Ashram i.e. the Celibacy Stage), and that he had recently started working as a teacher. Then he said that he wanted to marry Purnima with the permission and blessings of her parents.

Purnima's father could not believe this. He told his wife and Purnima about it. The stepmother became very happy to know that she will get rid of Purnima but at the same time she got extremely jealous of Purnima for getting such a nice husband. Purnima, though deaf and dumb, could understand what was said. Purnima readily and happily gave her consent. Purnima's father made it clear to the young man that the girl was deaf and dumb and had a permanent headache. But the young man did not change. After sometime, the young man – let us call him Shashi (the Moon) – and Purnima were duly married to each other. Purnima went to Shashi's house.

Shashi was a learned kind man. He always treated Purnima with respect and love. Through her gestures, when Purnima told Shashi on a Purnima Day (the Full Moon Day) that she had a headache, Shashi tried to give comfort and peace to her by very gently patting her head. Purnima felt a soothing relief thus far unknown to her. When Shashi was patting Purnima's head, his fingers struck against something hard. He was amazed. Looking closely through the thick long hairs, he found that there was a pin driven in her head. Very gently, so as not to hurt Purnima, Shashi pulled out the pin. Purnima heaved a sigh of relief. Then Shashi placed the pin on the table and they went to sleep.

When Shashi woke up next morning, he saw that the pin on the table had vanished and in its place there was a big sized diamond glittering in the shining rays of the beautiful morning Sun. Shashi was so surprised. Purnima was equally surprised but could not say anything; however, her lips did tremble a little.

After sometime, the same thing happened again; Shashi saw and pulled out a pin from Purnima's head, the pin vanished in the night, and the morning Sun brought them a big sized diamond.

Like this it happened again and again. Every time this happened, Purnima felt better and better. Gradually her sickly look disappeared totally and her face started glowing. Her blue eyes started twinkling. Her lips turned apple red. Her body skin turned pink. And, most importantly, her headache started declining and she started regaining her speech and hearing ability.

After eleven such episodes, Purnima's headache vanished totally and she became completely healthy, totally regaining her speech and hearing ability. They sold the diamonds. With the money thus received they constructed a beautiful house, set up the household, and saved the rest for future. Then they lived happily ever after with love and respect for each other. However, the saved money was never used because each day brought more and more of peace, happiness, and prosperity to them.

Undoubtedly, God has strange ways, and His love and mercy are boundless. Love in the family possesses unbelievable power; it can cure many diseases and it always brings in peace, happiness and prosperity.

NAAN - É – SHEERAZI

Once upon a time, perhaps about some four hundred years ago, there lived a man in a big town. He was a poor man. Nobody knew what his real name was. Since he was a poor man, really speaking, nobody ever bothered even to find out what his real name was; it is true, nobody cares about poor people what to say of their real names. Everybody used to call him Suleman though people knew that his real name was a long one.

Suleman used to live in a small hut on the outskirts of the big town where most of the poor people lived because being poor he did not have enough money to live in the expensive beautiful houses in the downtown or somewhere in the big town.

Suleman had come to the town from a far off land then known as Persia, now called as Iran. Actually Suleman had come to the town as a helper of a rich merchant from Persia. The rich merchant from Persia had heard a lot from others about the affluence of the country then known as Hindusthan, now called as India. The merchant, being an enterprising man, also wanted to try his luck. Yes, it is true, unless we try and make an effort, we cannot hope to achieve anything.

The merchant had come from Persia with a big convoy of camels carrying so many valuable things including some most beautiful carpets. He had a number of helpers with him. After staying in the town for sometime, the merchant was able to sell his goods at better prices than he had expected and earn a big profit. The rich people wanted to buy his things and they had plenty of money to do so. After he sold his goods, the merchant bought many goods from the town including cotton textiles, spices, dyes, etc. Being a shrewd businessman, he knew that these goods from India were then internationally famous and that he shall be able to sell these things at high prices in his homeland and earn a big profit again. When this was done, the rich merchant decided to return to Persia with his helpers.

Everyone who had come with the rich merchant wanted to go back as early as possible. They had started feeling nostalgic about their land, homes, and families and friends. There is no doubt that we miss our land, home, and family and friends all the more when we go away from them – absence makes the hearts grow fonder. Moreover everyone had also started feeling tired, having come after most tiring journey through desert, hills, and plains in scorching Sun, freezing cold and heavy rains on Camels, Horses and Bullock Carts. They also knew that they shall have to face the same on way back. But who can hope to achieve anything without working hard for it. Anyway. Briefly speaking, everyone wanted to go back. So did the rich merchant.

But Suleman did not want to go back. He wanted to stay in the town. When the rich merchant asked Suleman why he did not want to go back to Persia with others, Suleman revealed the secret. He had fallen in love with a beautiful girl in the town, his parents had died when he was still a child in Persia, he had no brothers or sisters, his uncles had already grabbed the family property, and they never liked to have any relationship with Suleman under the fear of a possible property dispute. Suleman added that he had liked the beautiful plains of India washed by rivers and rains every year making struggle for survival much easier and life more pleasant. Eventually the convoy left Suleman in the town and returned to Persia.

This is how Suleman, a poor young man from Persia, had come to live in the big town. Suleman had worked with the Persian merchant. Hence he had some idea about business matters. When Suleman decided to stay on in the big town, he started searching a job. This was not difficult. Suleman easily got a job as a helper with a local Seth (merchant) who used to sell textiles and carpets. The matter became easier for Suleman and the Seth not only because Suleman was familiar with that line of business but also because Suleman had been meeting that Seth when the Seth used to have dealings with the Persian merchant with whom Suleman used to work earlier. Thus Suleman got a job.

Suleman was a hard working and honest person. Hence, very soon he became a favorite of the Seth. Gradually his wages were raised. Seth also started involving him in some of his family matters. Suleman felt happy and settled.

Yes, Suleman felt happy and settled with a well-paid job and the beautiful loving wife who was none other than the girl he had fallen in love with. Yet sometimes he used to feel nostalgic about the village in Persia where he used to live as a child with his parents. He used to slide back deep in the memory of his childhood, his parents, his childhood friends, the games he played, the food he ate, the places he went, and so on. His wife was a wise and loving person. Whenever this happened, she used to give Suleman some time, and then distract his attention in a loving manner. Every day in the morning Suleman used to walk to his work in the downtown and return to his hut on the outskirts of the town in the evening. All was well.

One day the Seth told Suleman that he was going to have a big feast at his residence for family and friends and that he wanted to invite Suleman also for the same because Suleman had become so dear to him . Suleman thanked the Seth for the same and agreed humbly. The day and time for the feast was fixed.

Suleman went to the residence of the Seth. It was a huge gathering. The meals were served. They contained almost all the best dishes known to people at that time. Everybody enjoyed the feast. Suleman was also eating quietly in a corner.

To express his love and politeness, the Seth came to Suleman and asked him how the food was. Respectfully, but rather seriously, Suleman said that it was good. This gave the Seth an impression that perhaps Suleman did not like the food. So he again asked if he liked the food. Again, respectfully but rather seriously, Suleman said that he liked the food. Now the wise Seth could understand that there was certainly more than Suleman was saying out of his politeness.

The Seth asked Suleman to speak out frankly if the food was not good or if he did not like the food. Suleman said that the food was simply excellent but he still missed his Naan – É – Sheerazi.

The Seth was astonished to hear this. Somehow he had never heard of Naan – É – Sheerazi. He thought that Naan – É – Sheerazi must be some exquisite preparation *par excellence,* which he did not know about. The Seth kept quiet. The feast was over. Suleman returned to his home.

Suleman was a wise and intelligent person. Though the Seth had kept quiet on the moment, Suleman knew that he wanted to know what Naan – É – Sheerazi was. So after sometime Suleman most humbly requested the Seth to come to his residence for meals especially of Naan – É - Sheerazi. As if waiting for the moment, the Seth readily accepted the invitation. The day and time for the meals was fixed.

On the mutually agreed upon day and time, the Seth went to the hut of Suleman for meals of Naan – É – Sheerazi. On the ground a cotton sheet was spread for the Seth and Suleman to sit facing each other. In between the two, another piece of cloth was spread for the meals to be placed Suleman's wife placed lentil soup in two bowls – one for Suleman and the other for the Seth. Then she brought some thing duly wrapped in a piece of cloth and placed it on the ground in between the two. With this the meals to be served were served. Suleman told the Seth that it contained Naan – É – Sheerazi. He requested the Seth to kindly open the wrapper and start eating.

With suppressed but great excitement, the Seth opened the wrapping. It contained freshly baked wheat flour rotis (tortillas). The Seth looked at Suleman with great amazement and a clear question in his eyes.

Suleman clarified "Sir, the food served in your feast was simply excellent. However, this Naan – É – Sheerazi i.e. the Persian Bread is what I eat daily with the honest and limited means I have. I like it more than anything else in the world". When the Seth asked Suleman why it was so, Suleman said very politely "Sir, the excellent food you offered me was for one day only. But my humble food is available to me daily. If your food tempts me, I will start disliking my food. The result will be that either I will only get frustration and unhappiness or I will be tempted to resort to evil ways to get your food which will only lead me to prison someday". The wise Seth was overwhelmed with Suleman's wisdom and praised him for the same.

It is true that if we try to have what we cannot afford with our honest means then either it brings in unhappiness directly or leads us to crime which eventually leads to unhappiness.

Grandpa's Stories about India

THE FEROCIOUS HYENAS

NOTE: Based on real events around 1953

Strange and mysterious are the ways of God. At times He does what no one can easily comprehend or believe. God can fill the hearts of even the most cruel and merciless with abundant love and compassion. This is one such story. It is about hyenas.

Hyena is a carnivorous mammal of Asia and Africa allied to the dog. Hyenas are said to be not only dangerous but also most cunning and treacherous; they sneak in very quietly, attack their prey after an ambush, and run away very quickly with their theft. The present story about hyenas is based on real events, which occurred towards early 1950s in and around Lucknow.

Mythologically known as Lakshmanpur, established some seven thousand years ago by Lakshman, the younger brother of Lord Rama, Lucknow is located in the Indo-Gangetic plains of northern India. Now capital of the state of Uttar Pradesh (the northern state), Lucknow has been internationally renowned for centuries for its culture of refinement (called as Nafasat), politeness (called as Latafat), high thinking (called as Buland Khayali) and pursuit of excellence in all endeavors. But let us not sing odes about Lucknow. In short, Lucknow is a beautiful big city of north India. Naturally near and around it, there are many small towns. One of them is Sitapur.

Sitapur is a beautiful small town located about fifty miles to the north west of Lucknow on the verge of a forest, which extends up to the southern border of Nepal. Major events of this story occurred in a small village of Sitapur (for convenience, let us call it Bhanga) and the forest adjacent to it.

So the village of Bhanga was located on the border of Sitapur and the adjacent forest. It was a small village. Still many people used to live there. Their main occupation was agriculture and the allied activities included poultry farming, cattle rearing, dairying, etc. Since it was a small village, there was no electricity. Even police posts for providing safety and security to people were located far away. There was no train or bus facility and whenever needed, people used to travel by bullock carts.

Being located thus on the verge of a big forest, it was not uncommon for the forest animals and beasts to trespass into the village in search of food and water. The animals like elephants, deers, and bears used to come and graze in the adjacent agricultural fields sometimes causing severe damage to the crops . But beasts and other animals like lions, and hyenas used to pose a serious threat to the life of people and cattle in the village.

Once a lion invaded the village in the evening, killed, and lifted away a cow belonging to a poor farmer. It was too much of a loss for him. Cow was the only source of milk for him and his family and moreover he used the cakes made with cow-dung as fuel in the earthen stove at home. Then, there was a lion that had been badly injured due to the lack of skill of a hunter. He had thus lost the ability to kill animals and feed himself. So he had turned a man-eater. Once he killed a farmer who was returning home from the fields in the evening. The family lost its only breadwinner and found itself on the brink of starvation.

On another occasion, a couple of elephants entered the sugarcane field in the pitch dark of the night and completely destroyed the ready crop. This turned the owner to abject poverty as he could not repay the existing debts and had no money to meet the current family expenses.

Bears also used to cause damage to newly sown or ready to reap crops. However, the episodes related to lions, elephants, and bears were few.

But the large number of hyenas used to cause very frequent and serious damage. They would sneak in the dark of the night and take away the goat lambs, the cow calves, the chickens, etc. Since these used to be very important for the daily life of the people, they used to feel greatly disturbed. There had also been a few cases of great terror and sorrow in which the hyenas had stolen , killed, and eaten away human infants and toddlers. But hyenas, being rather small like dogs, were more difficult to guard against. The worst damage in that village by hyenas was done to the family of Shankar, a small farmer..

Actually it so happened that one day in the evening ,when it had started getting dark, Shankar returned home from the fields tired. He was lying on the bamboo cot inside the hut taking a little rest. His wife Parvati was milking the cow. Their only little son , let us call him Ganesh , a toddler of about eighteen months was playing on the ground near Parvati. Parvati had completed the milking chore. After a days hard work, she was also feeling tired. She picked up the pail containing milk and went inside the hut to keep it there.

In a couple of minutes, Parvati returned. But she was amazed to see that the little child was not there. Thinking that he may have crawled or toddled somewhere else, she started looking all around at first quickly and then almost madly. The child was not there. Not finding Ganesh, Parvati started crying and weeping bitterly. Hearing this, Shankar came out. Parvati told him what had happened. He too became nearly mad with shock and sorrow and he too started weeping bitterly.

The bitter and loud weeping sounds reached the neighbors. People from all directions ran to their hut apprehending that something serious had happened. When people asked what the matter was, Parvati and Shankar told them. Everybody joined together to look around.

Among these people, there was Bahadur. He was a middle-aged man. He used to accompany people coming to that area for hunting. So he had some idea about beasts and animals, their behavior, and footprints. With everybody else, Bahadur also looked around for the child. There was no success.

Suddenly, Bahadur saw some footprints on the wet ground near the back of the hut. The ground was wet there because in the absence of any drainage system, water used to collect there for sometime, then dry up , only to be followed by the arrival of new water used at home. Looking closely, Bahadur had no difficulty knowing what had happened.

With a very heavy heart and in a mournful voice he told everybody that some hyena had lifted away the little child Ganesh. This was more than anyone could tolerate. At once mournful weeping and crying started all around.

Picking up the hurricane lanterns containing kerosene oil, several people started running in all possible directions mostly toward the forest. Even after the most tiring efforts by all for several hours on that day, on the next day, and , then on the following day, nothing could be seen of the hyena who had lifted little Ganesh.

At last people slowed down the search effort till it came to a halt. Shankar and Parvati had no alternative but to take this as a God sent calamity. After sometime, they also resumed their daily routine with great pain in their hearts and permanent memory of Ganesh in their minds. For Parvati specially, it was difficult to reconcile with the truth. But what could be done.

Days, weeks, and months passed. Then, one day a miracle happened. It was quite common for the employees of the Forest Department of the State Government to go inside the forests from time to time and ensure that there was no unauthorized felling of trees and all was well.

When some employees of the Government were thus doing their job inside the deep forest, they heard a strange sound. Feeling amazed, they started moving in the direction from which they had heard the sound. Going a little distance, they saw something, which they could not believe. Inside a small cave, there was a human child lying on the ground. The sound they had heard had come from that child. Finding no other human being anywhere in close vicinity, they picked up the child.

The child was quickly brought to Sitapur, the District Headquarter. The news spread fast and wide like jungle fire. It reached the State Capital at Lucknow. The Government officials arranged to bring the child at once to Lucknow. The child was immediately admitted to Balrampur Hospital, the renowned Government owned Civil hospital at Lucknow.

The following days witnessed an unprecedented crowd of people visiting the Hospital to see the child, offer their blessings to him, and pray for him. People from all walks of life, in all age groups, and from near and far came to see the child. The hospital authorities had named him Ramu.

Ramu seemed to be a human child in all respects. However, instead of walking on his two feet, he used to walk around a little on all the four legs like animals . Further, Ramu did not speak like a human child. He used to produce throat sounds like hyenas. Ramu was in fact Ganesh, the little toddler of Shankar and Parvati who had been lifted away by hyena several months ago and who had been reared by hyena for months. Ramu came to be known as the Hyena Reared Human Child.

Ramu was a miracle. Hence, all possible efforts were made to save him. The best available brains, including those at the local King George's Medical College, were put to work to save the child. But in spite of all possible efforts, Ramu died after some months.

It is really a baffling irony of fate, which is as much surprising as shocking, that the best available human brains could not save a child who had been reared for months by ferocious carnivorous hyena.

Yes, strange and mysterious are the ways of God. At times He does what no one can easily comprehend or believe. God can fill the hearts of even the most cruel and merciless with abundant love and compassion.

Ram M. Saxena

THE WOOLEN FULL SLEEVE SWEATER

NOTE : True

Even to this day, I remember vividly that this happened in 1980. At that time, he was a kid of thirteen years. He had just graduated from Class VIII in the Government School at Almora (Almora is located in central Himalayas in the north west of India). His father wanted to send him for High School and Intermediate studies (called as High School in America) to one of the best Public Schools (called as Private Schools in America) in India. Though a man of rather modest means, his father had understood very clearly that the three best things which any parent could give to their children in the whole world were good life values, good health, and best available education.

But the task was not so easy. There was no such School in the town. However, the beautiful natural - lake city of Nainital was near enough at a distance of about forty miles (in hills, this is a long distance and one way journey takes three hours by not-comfortable buses moving at a snail's pace). Nainital had some of the finest Public Schools of the country mainly because starting with the British rule in India , it was the Summer capital of the State Government. . But the Boarding Public Schools were extremely expensive, much more expensive than what the boy's father could afford with his limited honest means. But eventually his father decided to spend everything he had (and borrow money if needed) but send him to the best School so that he could have a good future.

The father took him to Birla School (formerly known as Flender Smith School) in Nainital on July 5, 1980. After great hesitation the Principal told the father that there was only one seat available for admission to Class IX , that there were forty-five candidates for the same, and that it was going to be almost an exercise in futility for the child because there was no chance of admission. However, father was pleased that his son was allowed to appear at the Admission Test.

The Admission Test lasting two hours was held. The candidates were told to wait for the results. Some four or five teachers were deputed to assess the answer sheets. Assessment was done in about two hours. The result was announced. The boy had topped the list of all the candidates taking the test. He had been selected for admission to Class IX.

The father asked the Principal politely, though being a little apprehensive, what the fee was. The Principal called the Bursar who told the amount. The father took out a wad of currency notes from the pocket, which consisted of all he had. It was just enough to pay the fee fully. However, some thirty rupees i.e. about 60 cents (in the year 2002, one US $ = Rupees 50) remained with the father, which was enough to pay bus fare for the return journey of the father and the son.

When the father so readily paid the huge fee, the Principal was a little surprised. He asked how the father was so sure about the selection of his son. The father thanked the Principal but simply said that he had full faith in God and that he knew his son well. He added "Sir, I am sure this child will bring honor to your School someday". Then the two returned home.

The boy was asked to report for joining the School on July 15, 1980. He had also been given a very long list running into several sheets mentioning the items he was to bring with him when reporting for joining. It needed a lot of money. But somehow the father managed it. He went to the School and joined Class IX on July 15, 1980.

Days and weeks passed. Then came September 1980. There was a short Vacation of about a Week in the School and students were allowed to go home if they wanted to do so. He came home. His parents and ten year old sister were so happy and excited to see him, now a boarder in one of the best Public Schools of the country.

Though he was a very modest and non-demanding type, next day he told his mother that he would like to have a full sleeve woolen sweater if the family could afford it in terms of money. He said that he needed this to wear late in the evening when he used to go from his Boarding House to the Common Room to study until late in the night and when it used to be freezing cold at the altitude of 7700 ft above mean sea level where the School was located.

Though with a little pinch, mother bought the best woolen knitting yarn available in the local market and working almost non-stop with her affectionate hands, knitted the full sleeve woolen sweater before he boarded the bus for the return journey to the School. The short vacation was over.

Then came December 1980. It had already become unbearably cold at the School located at such a high altitude with snowfall every day and with virtually no heating arrangements. Like every year, the School was closed for Winter Vacation for three months. He came home for the Vacation.

Parents and the little sister were extremely glad to find him in their midst; this time they knew he shall be with them for a good time of three months.

One day the family was going out for an evening walk together. It was very cold. So everybody had a full sleeve woolen sweater and a woolen coat on. However, he was wearing only a sleeveless sweater and a coat. The parents took note of this but thought that perhaps he was not feeling so cold after living at an altitude of 7700 ft for months.

After a few days, the same thing happened again. The father asked him why he was not wearing his full sleeve woolen sweater. Very respectfully he said that he was fine. The matter ended.

He was never seen wearing his full sleeve woolen sweater with or without the coat be it morning, day or evening. The parents noted this.

One day his mother asked his father that she needed money to buy woolen yarn to knit a full sleeve woolen sweater for him (the son). Father felt a little annoyed because he was not using his first sweater and father could hardly afford the second sweater, which was not essential. Father was also amazed because his mother never made such unreasonable requests. He said so to his mother. And then the truth came out.

When asked by his mother, one day, why he was not wearing his full sleeve woolen sweater, he had told his mother thus "In September 1980 you had given that beautiful full sleeve woolen sweater to me as a present for my birthday on September 1. I liked it so much. I was wearing it with a woolen coat when I had left home to return to my School. When I reached Nainital I hired a porter to carry my luggage to my Boarding House in the School. As you know it is a long arduous uphill climb of about 1500 ft. Soon I saw that the porter was wearing only a tattered cotton shirt. Actually I was still feeling cold with a full sleeve woolen sweater, a woolen coat, and a woolen muffler on. So I thought that the poor porter must have been feeling miserable. I could not bear the sight. Hence I gave my full sleeve woolen sweater to that porter. I knew that father would be very angry.

Grandpa's Stories about India

But I could not prevent myself from doing that. I decided to bear the anger later on but helped the poor porter. Please forgive me for the same".

His mother was horrified and deeply pained to know that he had spent all the time from September to early December in the freezing cold in the School without the full sleeve woolen sweater. After knowing this, on that very day, she wanted to buy woolen yarn to knit another full sleeve woolen sweater for him.

When the mother narrated the story to the father, the father told their son "We are proud of you. What you did was the right thing. You, however, did a wrong. You did not tell us about it and suffered the cold. That has given pain to our hearts. If we knew about it, somehow, we would have got another full sleeve woolen sweater for you and got it delivered to you in the School itself. Remember this for future". Needless to say, another full sleeve woolen sweater was knitted and given to him in no time, this time, not as a birthday present but as a prize for the kind deed he had done.

It is my observation and belief that God showers His unlimited bliss on good people. With God's blessings and his own hard work, the kid mentioned in this story became very successful ; he continues to be kind and sharing . He is now an Engineer in the USA. He has a beautiful loving wife who is a physician. As I am recording this story on computer, their one-year-old son Dave is playing in the adjacent family room in a cabin in Flagstaff, which is their vacation home. The twinkle of love in his eyes and the honest smile on his little sweet lips tells me that Dave will be as kind and sharing as his father. Amen.

If still you have not been able to guess, then I am pleased and honored to say that this is the story of my son, Sumeet.

Ram M. Saxena

THE KIND-HEARTED WOODCUTTER

He was a poor man. He used to live in a small cottage in a small town. The town was situated on the edge of a forest. He used to earn his livelihood by going to the forest daily in the morning, cutting branches of the trees there, making a bundle of the same, carrying them as a head-load to the market, and selling them so as to earn some money and buy the things needed by the family for their daily life. Though poor, he was a religious and a kind man.

One day in the morning when he was on his way to the forest, he saw some hunters going to the forest. This was not uncommon in those days. Rich people and people belonging to the ruling elite used to amuse themselves at times with hunting. The woodcutter did not pay much attention to the event or to the people and concentrated his mind and energies on his own work as a good honest man should do.

However, after two days, the woodcutter saw those people again. This time, it was in the town itself. The hunters had stopped at a restaurant and they were most happily enjoying their meals. Outside the restaurant, there were two bullock carts. Looking closely inside the bullock carts, the woodcutter saw two dead lions, one in each cart. He noticed that one was a lion with thick manes on the back of the neck and the other was a lioness without such manes. Again, this was not an unknown event. It used to happen sometimes. What was death for the forest animals was entertainment for the hunters. But that was the way life and things were in those times. So the woodcutter went his way and the hunters, after the meals, theirs.

Next day, the woodcutter went to the forest as usual. Going a little distance, he heard a groan – a low deep sound of pain. He went in the direction of the sound. Going a little distance, he saw that a very small lion cub was there in a small pit full of thorns. The thorns were hurting him and, hence, he was groaning. The more he was trying to come out, the more the thorns hurt him.

The woodcutter stopped to think. After thinking carefully for sometime, he felt certain that the cub was the offspring of the lion and the lioness killed by the hunters a couple of days ago. The woodcutter thought that if he left the cub there itself, then some other animal would kill him. Or unable to feed himself, the cub shall die of hunger.

In any case, the cub was sure to die. Being a kind man, the woodcutter felt mercy on the cub and decided to rescue him.

Carefully, the woodcutter cut some of the branches of the thorns with his axe. Then, very tenderly and carefully, he picked up the cub, all the time patting him gently on the head, the neck, the back, and everywhere. Then he wrapped the little cub in his turban (the long head wear of cloth) and carried him on his back. Apparently the cub was too weak to resist. And again, perhaps he had seen the love and mercy in the behavior of the woodcutter.

The woodcutter picked up some wood and then returned home. When he reached home, his wife was too shocked to see the cub. When the woodcutter narrated the entire story, as a human being and that too a woman, she started feeling love for the cub. The cub was chained to a nearby tree. The woodcutter and his wife began treating the cub as their own child; feeding him with whatever they could spare, patting him fondly, and thus comforting him.

When the neighbors saw that there was a cub next door, they got so scared. Though a small cub, he was still a lion. Whenever he used to give his little roar, it used to be still frightening. Anyone and everyone who came to know about the cub admonished the woodcutter and his wife to get rid of the cub as soon as possible. A few days passed thus. Seeing that the cub was still there, the neighbors started blaming and even fighting with the woodcutter and his wife. They wanted the cub removed at once.

But it was almost as difficult to remove the cub as to keep him. He could not be let loose like stray cats or dogs. And he could not be returned to the forest because he was still too young to protect or feed himself. But the problem was solved easily one day. It so happened that a merchant was passing through the street on which the woodcutter had his cottage. The merchant was too amazed to see a beautiful live cub tied to a tree. When he asked people around, he learnt the entire story. Being a shrewd businessman, he thought of a nice way out.

The merchant told the woodcutter that he was prepared to take the cub with him if only the woodcutter would permit. He further assured the woodcutter and his wife that he should take full care of the cub and no harm whatsoever shall befall the cub. The woodcutter and his wife had developed enormous love for the cub. So they felt deep sorrow while parting with the cub. Seeing this, the shrewd merchant gave them some money as a consolation. Though the woodcutter's wife did not want to accept any money, the woodcutter eventually accepted the money. The cub left the woodcutter's cottage.

Days rolled into weeks, weeks into months, and months into a couple of years. Nothing worth mentioning happened. However, one night, when the woodcutter and his family were fast asleep, they heard a loud sound of something falling on the thatched roof of the cottage, breaking the roof and then falling inside the cottage. Everyone got up at once. Lighting a small oil lamp, the woodcutter saw what had fallen through the broken roof. It was something tied in a big piece of cloth. The woodcutter opened the wrapping. At once, the cottage was filled with the glitter of the diamonds, other gems, and gold jewelry, which was there in the wrapping.

For a moment, the woodcutter and his wife felt happy and thought of retaining the windfall. But the next moment their consciences made them feel guilty because they were all honest people. It was decided that next morning the jewelry should be handed over to the police. Everyone prepared to return to sleep.

They had not even lied down on the ground where they slept when again they heard loud sounds. This time the sounds were those of horses and several men talking to each other loudly. Then, there was a knock on the door. The woodcutter got up and opened the door.

Before the woodcutter could speak anything, the soldiers arrested him. Then they entered the cottage, looked around and spotted the cloth wrapping in a corner. Opening it, they saw the jewelry. They picked up the jewelry. Then they left with the prisoner and the jewelry. The woodcutter's wife tried to protest and explain but none bothered even to listen to her.

Next morning the case was presented in the court of the King. The Chief of the soldiers said that during the previous night there had been a theft in the palace of the King. The soldiers had chased the thieves. But the thieves had eventually disappeared in the dark of the night near the cottage of the woodcutter. This had created doubts in the minds of the soldiers. So they had entered the cottage of the woodcutter, recovered the jewelry, and arrested the woodcutter. Under the circumstances, woodcutter was the thief. According to law everywhere, he who possesses the stolen goods is the thief unless and until he can reveal the real thief.

The King felt very angry with the man who could dare to steal from the royal palace. The King decided to punish the prisoner – the woodcutter – in such a manner that in future no one would dare even to think of stealing from the royal palace. The King ordered that on the fifth day, the prisoner shall be left unarmed before the King's pet lion that shall be kept hungry in the meantime so that the lion kills him mercilessly. The poor woodcutter tried his best but under the situation no one believed a word of what he said. He was thrown into the prison.

On the fifth day, a huge crowd gathered to watch the punishment. There was a big area surrounded by walls on all the sides with huge windows so that people could see inside. The poor woodcutter was brought and left in the enclosure. Then the King ordered for the hungry lion to be brought to the enclosure. The lion was brought and let loose in the enclosure. Everybody watching was horrified knowing that the hungry lion will tear the prisoner to pieces. The huge lion roared. Then the lion moved to the man in anger as if to kill him.

But then there was a miracle. The lion went near the woodcutter, smelled him, and licked the woodcutter's hands. Scared to death, the woodcutter fell on the ground. After a few moments, the lion stretched himself on the ground besides the woodcutter, started licking the hands of the woodcutter , rubbing his neck against the woodcutter's body and wagging his tail like a pet dog. Everybody present was surprised beyond limits. None could believe his eyes.

However, the King was a wise man. He asked everyone present if this could be explained. But none could say a word. The King developed some doubts. He asked the soldiers to take the lion back to his cage and give him some food. Then he ordered the soldiers to bring the woodcutter to him. When the prisoner was brought, the King asked him to speak out the truth and told him that if he spoke the truth, the King shall pardon him irrespective of whatever he had done.

The woodcutter spoke the truth. He told the King how the royal jewelry had reached him, how he wanted to return it to the King, and how he was arrested before he could do anything. Then he told the King that most probably the lion was the same cub that the woodcutter had rescued and reared for sometime. The merchant who had bought the cub from the woodcutter and sold the same to the King at a good profit confirmed the facts. The King pardoned the woodcutter and released him after a suitable reward for his kindness to the cub that was now a favorite pet lion of the King.

In the meantime, King's men caught the real thieves and put them in the prison for King's justice. Then onwards the King never gave life sentence to anybody because in some cases truth COULD take sometime to come out.

The woodcutter showed kindness to the cub. The cub, now a fully-grown lion , returned the kindness to the woodcutter. In our real lives, we come across many people who prove to be ungrateful; instead of remembering and returning the kindness extended to them, they even go to the extent of harming their benefactor. Sometimes one starts wondering if some animals and even beasts are better than some human beings.

Whatever one thinks on certain moments, the story of the kind-hearted woodcutter tells us that in the end, the truth always prevails and God certainly blesses those people with His love and mercy who are kind to others – animals or humans.

THE ROYAL HORSE

NOTE : The main events on which the story is based are true and were narrated to me by my Friends at Jodhpur

Rajasthan, formerly known as Rajputana, is located on the western border of India. Beyond Rajasthan there is the Thar desert and then there is Pakistan. Rajasthan is apparently divided into two parts by the Shivalik mountains viz the eastern part which gets regular rains and hence which is green, and the western part which gets very scanty rains and hence most of which is desert and arid. Jodhpur is located in the western part and largely it consists of arid desert land. However, when the Sun sets, the cool breeze blows through the Keekar trees and sand produces a very sweet sound; it appears as if the desert has suddenly come to life and it is singing. Listening to that music and feeling that cool breeze on one's body, after a very hot day of scorching Sun, is a heavenly experience.

But the main purpose of this story is not to sing songs in the praise of the beauty of Jodhpur. So let us return to our story.

Before the merger of the princely states into the Indian Union in 1948, Jodhpur was the capital of the erstwhile State of Marwar. Though entire Rajasthan (including in particular the princely states of Jaipur and Udaipur) has been famous for centuries for its great heroes, the State of Marwar has been uniquely renowned worldwide for its chivalrous rulers possessing qualities of dignity, courtesy, bravery, generosity, and gallantry. The brave rulers of Jodhpur are perhaps best described by the phrase RAN BANKA RATHORE in Marwari dialect, which means the extremely fierce warriors. One of these great rulers was King Umed Singh. The events mentioned in this story occurred when King Umed Singh was the ruler, i.e. some time in the 1930s.

So King Umed Singh was the ruler of Jodhpur at that time. He was a very wise, brave, religious, honest, and kind man. He took enormous pains to undertake activities and implement programs, which benefited the masses. He built the exquisite Umed Palace, the Jodhpur Railway Station, the Jodhpur Airport, the General Hospital, the Women's Hospital, the two postgraduate colleges, the girls' degree college, the Public Park, the Zoo, roads, public water system, and so much more. It is not possible to present an all-inclusive list here. For doing all this, he was greatly loved and revered by his people.

But it can be easily understood that one man alone could not have done so much of good work; naturally he needed helpers. His most important helper was his brother Sir Pratap Singh.

Sir Pratap was a very wise, an exceptionally brave, and a kind man. He was greatly respected and loved by his people. Even the British rulers (India was ruled by the British at that time and became Independent on August 15, 1947 just as America became Independent on July 4, 1776) were so impressed by him that the British Government conferred knighthood on him and hence he was called as "Sir" Pratap. On the one hand, Sir Pratap was known for his kindness for the needy but on the other hand he was also known for his strictness against the wicked and the bad. Therefore, it was only natural that the wicked and the bad did not like Sir Pratap.

Though Sir Pratap knew that some bad people did not like him and were always on the look out of a suitable opportunity to harm him, if possible kill him, he was too brave and too good to be scared of them. He used to move around freely throughout the State trying to find out the things at the grass root level.

Once it so happened that Sir Pratap had gone out of the royal palace on his usual visit to some remote parts of the State. He was riding his horse, a most beautiful spotless white horse that affectionately he used to call DHAURIA (the White Beauty). Though Sir Pratap had a large number of helpers to take care of the horse, he used to spend sometime every day to pat and pamper the horse. He loved the horse and the horse loved him.

Riding his horse in a most graceful and brisk manner, Sir Pratap was returning to Jodhpur. On way, he was passing through a forest. Suddenly he found that some twenty people surrounded him with naked swords in their hands and faces covered with black cloth so as not to be recognized. A warrior of enormous experience, Sir Pratap took no time to understand that they were determined to kill him. Perhaps, Sir Pratap could try to escape by running away. But he was a brave Rajput. Even to this day, there is a tradition among Rajputs that neither they show their back to the enemy nor they attack the back of an enemy; brave Rajputs fight face to face.

The fight started. Sir Pratap was a very courageous and skilled warrior. He hurt many of them and even killed some of them. However, good and brave people often commit a mistake. Being good and brave themselves they start presuming that the others shall behave likewise. But wicked and bad cannot behave thus. Though Sir Pratap was fighting wonderfully well, he could hardly visualize that some cowards shall attack him from the back. The attack was so sudden and powerful on the back of his head that he fell from the horse on the ground. This made the task of the assailants much easier. They injured Sir Pratap seriously. Then they left hoping that Sir Pratap shall die of bleeding or being in a seriously wounded condition shall be killed by some wild beast.

Dhauria, the royal horse, was watching all this. He could understand that if Sir Pratap was left all alone in the forest then the wishes of the assailants shall be fulfilled – either death by bleeding or at the hands of some beast. He decided to do something.

Dhauria grabbed the cummerbund (a broad sash worn as a belt) of Sir Pratap with his teeth and lifted him. Then as fast as he could make it, he ran to the royal palace in Jodhpur. Dhauria arrived late in the evening. He placed the body of unconscious Sir Pratap on the ground and neighed very loudly.

Though it was dark , there were people around. When they heard the enormous neighing of the horse at that hour , they were amazed. Then they heard it again. Now it was certain that there was something wrong somewhere.

Several people came running from different directions to the place where Dhauria was standing. Coming near, they saw the body of Sir Pratap soaked in blood from head to toe. At once it became clear that he had been attacked by some bad people, hurt very seriously, and the royal horse had rescued him to the royal palace.

The best available medical care was provided to Sir Pratap. He took sometime to be normal because the injuries were extremely serious but being a brave and strong man, he recovered much faster. After sometime, he was healthy again.

Sir Pratap always loved Dhauria and Dhauria always loved him. Sir Pratap could be saved only because of the wisdom and effort of the royal horse. More than being a royal horse, Dhauria was a LOYAL horse.

Ram M. Saxena

    If we love animals then they love us and can be of unbelievable help under some situations. So we should love animals also.

Grandpa's Stories about India

JATNI'S ADMONITION

NOTE : The main events on which the story is based are true and were narrated to me by my friends at Jodhpur

Right from his youth, King Jodha Singh was a man of extraordinary bravery and enterprise. Around the year 1450, he founded the beautiful city of Jodhpur in Rajasthan, then known as Rajputana. With his benign support and imagination, soon people started prospering under his rule.

However, in those days (is it not true even today ?) it was common for kings to attack other states and try to enlarge their own kingdoms. When the King of Jodhpur concentrated his focus on development and welfare, the task of security and defense got a little neglected. Soon he had to pay a price for the same.

Some enemies of King Jodha within the state joined hands with his enemies outside the state and rebelled against him. Taken totally unaware, King Jodha could not resist much. He fought gallantly but eventually he had to flee Jodhpur.

Even though King Jodha left Jodhpur he could not forget his beloved city. Traveling to places where he had friends and from whom he could expect help and support, King Jodha reorganized his army. He attacked Jodhpur. The battle was fought bravely. But he got defeated. He had to run away. He reorganized the whole thing again, attacked Jodhpur again but had to meet the same result.

This happened several times. The result was that people started developing doubts about King Jodha's fighting and leading abilities. His friends started hesitating to provide him support. Many of his trusted men deserted him. He became a lonely man.

What an irony of fate ? Once the founding father and King of Jodhpur, King Jodha had to hide himself in a forest. But even in the forest, it was not safe and relaxed for him. His enemies knew that he was hiding somewhere in the forest and hence their soldiers were constantly in search of him. He had to constantly move from place to place. And all the time, he had to wear a disguise lest he is recognized, caught, and killed.

Thus King Jodha was passing through the worst circumstances of his life. But he was a wise man. He knew that fortune-misfortune, gain-loss, honor-ignominy, and life-death are in the hands of God and hence instead of losing heart, he should keep doing his duty. That meant efforts to reorganize his army, attack Jodhpur, and recapture his lost kingdom.

One day, when King Jodha was roaming in the forest, all alone, duly disguised, he felt hungry. He started looking around. After going some distance, he saw a cottage. The door of the cottage was open. There was an old woman, sitting by the side of the Chulha (earthen stove in which wood is used as fuel) and cooking Bajra Rotis (Tortillas).The smell of the food was most inviting and hunger was too compelling. King Jodha went to the door of the cottage.

It was a cottage of a Jat farmer. The old Jat woman (Jatni) was the mother of the Jat farmer. Jats have been known as great farmers and warriors and their practical wisdom is said to be matchless; particularly, Jatnis are said to possess exceptional wisdom.

King Jodha paid his respectful greetings to the Jatni. The Jatni said some words of blessings. Then she asked him what did he want. He asked if it was possible for him to get some food. The Jatni, being a kind hearted person following the typical tradition of treating the guests, asked him to wash his hands and sit down on the bare floor of the cottage. The King obeyed.

The Jatni gave some peeled and cut onion to the King and told him to wait for the Bajra Roti. Then she cooked a fresh Bajra Roti and on a piece of cloth served it to the King. The King was very hungry. The moment Bajra Roti was placed on the piece of cloth in front of him, he poked his index finger in the middle of the Roti. But he had to withdraw his finger immediately; it had sustained a near burn because the Roti was full of steam and very hot. To sooth his finger, King Jodha placed it in his mouth.

Watching this amusingly, the Jatni started laughing . Laughing hard she said "You seem to be King Jodha". The King was totally shocked with surprise. For a moment he thought that he had been recognized. But the next moment he was confident. He was wearing such a disguise that even if his own family members had seen him thus, they would not have been able to recognize him. Certainly the Jatni , a total stranger, had not recognized him. The matter was something else.

Maintaining his composure and serenity, the King asked her respectfully why did she say that. The Jatni replied "You want to eat the Roti. It is steaming hot. You put your finger in its middle and burn it. You should start breaking it from the edge. The steam shall go out, the Roti shall cool down, and you shall be able to eat. King Jodha is committing the same blunder. He wants to conquer Jodhpur. But instead of conquering the adjoining areas first and then attacking Jodhpur, he is attacking Jodhpur straightaway. The result is that he is wasting his time and valuable men and material. Hence, I called you King Jodha".

King Jodha did not say anything but simply kept quiet. After the meals, he thanked the Jatni, touched her feet as a mark of respect, and then left.

The old Jatni had admonished him enough. With renewed vigor, King Jodha once again reorganized his army. He started attacking and conquering the peripheral areas of Jodhpur. Each victory brought him added strength and confidence, as well as respect and support from others. Soon King Jodha launched a full-scale attack on Jodhpur. The enemies were no match to King Jodha's chivalry. Jodhpur was conquered and the kingdom was regained.

As soon as he settled down, King Jodha searched out the old Jatni, told her the entire story, thanked her profoundly, and gave her plenty of presents to express his gratitude. Then he ruled the kingdom for many years.

The story tells us that we should never underestimate others. Even a most ordinary person in the street can give us valuable ideas. Hence, we should always keep an open mind and listen to others with respect.

Ram M. Saxena

GAJA GHALE

NOTE : The story is based on facts narrated to me by people at Almora

Almora is located in the central Himalayas in the northwest of India at an altitude of about 5500 ft above Mean Sea Level. Before 1815, it was a part of the Kingdom of Nepal . In the year 1815, a battle was fought between the British India Army (at that time India was under the British rule) and the Nepalese army . It is known as the Battle of Sitholi. This is so because the battle was fought in the forest-village of Sitholi. (The forest-village of Sitholi is perched on the hills on the northern side of Almora. When I was in Almora, every evening, from the balcony of my house , I could see the unobstructed and enchanting view of the evening Sun rays turning into gold the snow covered peaks – Nanda Devi, Trishul, Panch Chuli, and Chaukhambha , and bathing the Sitholi forest-village, and the city of Almora below it with their liquid gold.)

To resume our story, the British Indian Army won the battle leading to the Treaty of Sitholi. It was pursuant to the provisions of this Treaty that Almora became a part of British India, now free India. Later Almora became known worldwide , thanks to the most fascinating hunting tales written by Jim Corbett and known as the Man Eaters of Kumaon; Almora is located in the heart of Kumaon. In 1815, the first Gorkha Regiment was raised in Almora.

Gaja Ghale was then a teenaged boy of Almora. He had a strong character, a very healthy body, an alert mind, and a strong will to do something good in life. But coming from a rather poor family and possessing virtually no resources, he wondered what he could do. God helps those who help themselves. Hence, God found a way for Gaja Ghale.

On June 28, 1914 Archduke Francis Ferdinand, heir to the Austrian – Hungarian throne, and his wife, were murdered. Soon Austria – Hungary declared war on Serbia. Then Germany declared war on Russia and France. Then England declared war on Germany (now India , then under the British rule, was on war). Later other nations became involved. This was the beginning of the First World War.

As soon as the War started, large-scale recruitment was made to the Indian Army. Gaja Ghale joined the Indian Army as a soldier. Now he was to fight, as an Indian soldier, on behalf of the British Government.

Gaja Ghale was provided some initial training. Then he was sent to the front. He was sent to many places to fight. He fought courageously and bravely everywhere. Then he became a member of the British fighting force in France, fighting the German forces.

The German army was constantly trying to attack and capture the crucial outpost where Gaja Ghale was posted. Though the Indian soldiers were fighting with all the skill and courage, it was apparent that the Germans had an upper hand. Gaja Ghale's unit had been fighting for several days. Every soldier had become greatly tired. Gradually it had become clear that unless some additional force and relief was provided, the outpost could be lost. This was not acceptable, neither to the officers nor to the brave soldiers and certainly not to Gaja Ghale.

One day it so happened that the Commanding Officer had to go somewhere for something more pressing. He called Gaja Ghale and told him that till the Officer's return, Gaja Ghale was In-Charge of the Outpost. He warned Gaja Ghale to be alert round the clock as the German soldiers could attack anytime. He further promised that he was going to arrange for relief and additional force. A brave and dedicated soldier, Gaja Ghale saluted the Officer with a "Yes, Sir" and took charge of the Outpost. The Officer left.

Two days passed. Nothing happened. But the third night proved to be dangerous and eventful. In the pitch dark of the night, the German soldiers attacked. Gaja Ghale and his men fought courageously and bravely. But they were much fewer than required. Moreover, they were also tired. On the other hand, the German unit was a large one and also a fresh one. Some of Gaja Ghale's men were injured. He arranged for their removal to a safer place. Everyone kept fighting.

Then suddenly a bullet in the shoulder hit Gaja Ghale. But he took no note of it. He kept guiding his men and fighting himself. One of his men saw the blood oozing from Gaja Ghale's shoulder. He had no difficulty in understanding that a bullet had hit Gaja Ghale. He also knew that unless Gaja Ghale was removed quickly to a safer place and medical treatment was provided to him, the injury could become fatal. He requested Gaja Ghale repeatedly to go. But Gaja Ghale refused to do so. His reply was "How can I go? How can I leave the Outpost? How can I leave my men ?".

Just as Gaja Ghale was about to faint, his Officer returned. He also brought not only relief but also additional force as planned and promised. The moment Gaja Ghale saw his Officer he said "Sir" and fainted.

After a couple of days Gaja Ghale regained his consciousness in a hospital. He was told that the battle he was fighting had been won; the Outpost had been retained. He was also happy to see that everybody around was extremely happy and impressed with him. He had become a great Hero.

Eventually at 11 A.M. on November 11, 1918 the First World War ended. The story of Gaja Ghale's bravery and dedication to duty even at the risk of his life had traveled far and wide; it had reached even England.

The British Government decided to award Gaja Ghale VICTORIA CROSS, the highest military honor of the then British Empire – the Empire where the Sun did not set. He was also awarded some land and money.

I had the privilege and the honor of meeting Gaja Ghale at Almora. He is a simple and a modest man. When asked he only says" I just did my

Duty"; surely this reminds one of General Nelson.

The story reveals that even a small man can get highest honors in the World only if he does his duty with full concentration using all the ability and skill he has.

Grandpa's Stories about India

NO DISTRACTIONS, PLEASE

NOTE : Very often, this was one of the three stories narrated by my late mother after special prayers when I was a child

Thousands of years ago, once Lord Shiva, the God of Destruction according to Hindu mythology, was gracing his seat atop Mount Kailash. To his left was seated his beloved wife Goddess Parvati. His two worthy sons God Ganesha and God Kartikeya were also seated nearby.

Seeing Lord Shiva a little thoughtful, Goddess Parvati asked respectfully what was he thinking. Lord Shiva replied that for long he had not been able to go round the World and find out for himself how the things were going on everywhere. He added that hence he was thinking of going on a visit to the World.

Goddess Parvati was too pleased to hear this. She knew that Lord Shiva was known as BHOLE BABA (the Pure Hearted Father) everywhere in the World .He was too kind a person to say No to anybody who offered his respects to him, worshipped him, and asked for favors irrespective of whether he was a good man or a bad man. With his blessings, Lord Shiva had obliged both, Lord Rama and Demon Ravana. She knew that if he goes to the World, he will do only good to some people. She thought of going with Lord Shiva to witness the blessing events.

Goddess Parvati asked Lord Shiva if she could also go with him. Lord Shiva said "My beloved Goddess Parvati. I will be most happy to take you along with me. But as you know, the visit to the World will not be a happy one. In this World, due to their past evil deeds, human beings suffer in various ways. You are an extremely kind person with motherly love for the whole World. You will not be able to withstand their misery. So better stay here and let me go alone".

But Goddess Parvati wanted to go. Therefore, she repeated her request. Lord Shiva tried to make her understand again. But it seems Goddess Parvati had already made up her mind and, hence, she was determined to go. She insisted on going. At last Lord Shiva said "If you are so keen on going with me, then let it be so".

Lord Shiva climbed his bull Nandi. Goddess Parvati sat behind him. Then they left Mount Kailash for the World.

Traveling through the most bewitching permanently snow-covered peaks they came down . They entered the lush green forests. The forest animals were most delighted to see Lord Shiva (Lord Shiva is also known as PASHUPATINATH which means the Lord of the Animals) accompanied by his wife Goddess Parvati. They greeted them in the best of their ways. The lions roared, the elephants trumpeted , the wild horses neighed, the donkeys brayed, the bears danced, the deers hopped, the pigs oinked, the birds chirped and twittered, and so on. Accepting their greetings and giving their blessings to all of them , Lord Shiva and Goddess Parvati moved on.

Moving on, Lord Shiva and Goddess Parvati atop Nandi, enjoyed the matchless beauty of the beautiful green forests and the singing waterfalls inside them. They halted here and there but only briefly; as we all know, it is not wise to stop here and there unnecessarily when one is going somewhere for some specific purpose.

Traveling long distances thus, Lord Shiva and Goddess Parvati entered the human World. Lord Shiva warned Goddess Parvati that there were all sorts of people in the World – good and bad, honest and deceptive, rich and poor, happy and unhappy – and hence the best thing for her would be to keep quiet and let him handle his affairs. Goddess Parvati promised that she will comply with the admonition. They moved on.

When they went some distance, they saw that a big beautiful house was aflame. People near it were trying to extinguish the fire but it was too strong and it was apparent that the house shall be reduced to ashes soon. There was a man standing near it and he was weeping bitterly. When the man saw Lord Shiva and Goddess Parvati, then he grabbed their feet and asked them for mercy. Lord Shiva kept quiet. But Goddess Parvati's motherly heart started melting. In a low voice, which no one could hear, she requested Lord Shiva to save the house and revert it to its original beautiful condition. Lord Shiva knew that the man had built the house with immorally earned money and hence God was punishing him. Hence, he did not want to interfere. But Goddess Parvati insisted. Eventually Lord Shiva obliged. They moved on.

Going some distance again, they met a handsome man. The man seemed to be a brave warrior. But he was sitting on the side of a street

Grandpa's Stories about India

in the hope of some alms. When he saw Lord Shiva and Goddess Parvati riding Nandi, he came forward and grabbed their feet. Lord Shiva asked him what was the matter and what did he want from them. The man said that his name was Veer Singh, that he used to be a King, that his best friend had betrayed him and captured his Kingdom, that he wanted to kill him, and that with great difficulty he had been able to save his life and run away. He requested Lord Shiva and Goddess Parvati to bless him and restore his Kingdom. Lord Shiva knew that the man was being punished for what he had done in his previous birth and, hence, he did not want to interfere. But here again the plight and request of the man moved Goddess Parvati. Much against his wishes Lord Shiva had to restore the man's Kingdom. Then he hinted Nandi and they moved on fast.

As they traveled, Lord Shiva and Goddess Parvati kept quiet. But when they had traveled some distance, they found that there was a woman sitting on the side of the street with apparently a child in her lap. This was no amazing sight. However, as the woman saw Lord Shiva and Goddess Parvati, she shouted and requested them to halt for a moment only. Lord Shiva rode on but Goddess Parvati requested him to stop for a moment and listen to what the woman was saying. So they stopped.

The woman said that her only child was very sick and she would be most grateful if only Goddess Parvati would touch the child with the little finger in her left hand so as to heal him. A simple kind lady with enormous motherly love, Goddess Parvati saw no harm in so doing. The moment Goddess Parvati touched the so-called child wrapped in a cloth, the woman threw the bundle of cloth and started screaming that Goddess Parvati had killed her only child.

Everybody near and far started wondering and blaming Goddess Parvati, who was totally amazed with the happening. The woman flung herself in front of Nandi. She said that she would not allow Lord Shiva and Goddess Parvati to move even an inch unless and until her child was restored to life. Feeling greatly sorry about what had happened, Goddess Parvati requested Lord Shiva to help. Lord Shiva knew the truth.

Actually that woman had no child. She was too keen to have one. So she had asked one fortune-teller as to what she should do to have a child. The fortune-teller had told her that on such and such day and time, Lord Shiva and Goddess Parvati would travel through this street. He had also told the woman to make an effigy of a boy with gram-floor, dress it up like a boy, hold it in her arms, ask Goddess Parvati to touch it with the little finger of her left hand, start screaming and blaming Goddess Parvati that she had killed her child hearing which Lord Shiva will give life to the effigy.

But under the situation Lord Shiva found no way out. So he touched the so-called child with the little finger of his left hand and said "Get Up". The boy at once got up to life. The woman thanked them and went away.

Then Lord Shiva thought of returning to Mount Kailash. The moment he thought of it, he found himself and Goddess Parvati atop Mount Kailash in the midst of God Ganesh and God Kartikeya with Nandi seated in front of them.

This story is a complete myth. However, it has an important message. When we do some work, we should do it with full concentration using all our ability and skill without any distraction.

Grandpa's Stories about India

UNITED WE STAND

David used to live in a small town of Nagaland near Kohima with his wife Kim, two children and old parents. Nagaland is located on the northeastern border of India adjoining China. He was a farmer. He was neither rich nor poor. He was a good sincere Christian. So was his wife Kim. They had less than average height, light bodies, and beige (ecru) skin color (more like light yellow) due to the local conditions in that part of India. They were well to do; neither rich nor poor.

On that particular day, David and Kim were feeling a little tired after a day's hard work. So completing the daily family chores, they said their prayers, and went to sleep. They had a sound sleep. However, during the night, David saw a strange dream.

David saw that he was praying in the Church of Mother Mary all-alone. While so doing, it seemed to him that the lips of the beautiful statue of Mother Mary opened a little. Not only this, it seemed to him that he also heard a sweet kind voice. For a moment he thought that it was only his misunderstanding; how could a statue of marble speak. But then he wondered if his eyes and ears both could go wrong and that too at the same time. Being a religious man, he had heard of heavenly miracles. Hence he gathered a little courage and respectfully asked "Holy Mother, did you say something "/ The statue in front of him spoke again "Yes, my son. What do you want"? David was too happy to hear the kind sweet voice of Mother Mary. He said that he wanted his wife Kim to be cured of the mysterious killing disease, which could not be cured despite all efforts and a little more money to be able to live peacefully. The Holy Mother simply said "Nagpur. Ramgarh. Umaria. Golden Hill. Go". When David looked again, the statue was silent and all was the same as it used to be for years. David got very excited. Out of excitement, he woke up.

Kim was sleeping by his side; her face looked very peaceful and she had a smile on which David had not seen for long due to the serious disease she was suffering with. David did not disturb her. But soon Kim also got up. It was rather early in the morning, say about 4 AM. David and Kim spoke simultaneously "I saw a dream". They were both astonished to hear each other. Then David asked Kim to narrate her dream. When Kim narrated her dream, David was all the more surprised. She had seen and heard in her dream exactly what he had seen and heard in his dream. After talking to each other briefly they both agreed that the dream was more likely to be true since both of them had seen it simultaneously and that too in the holy morning hours. They also decided to follow the instructions given to them in the dream because in spite of all the efforts, Kim was losing her health gradually and it was rather clear that if this continued, she might not live for long. So arranging some money some how, they decided to go. There was no harm in trying this last resort. Just in case it did work.

David and Kim boarded the train at Kohima. Then, they came to Calcutta. From there, they took another train and reached Nagpur. They had already found that the little town of Ramgarh was 143 miles to the north of Nagpur. One could go there by bus. Since it was already late in the afternoon, they decided to stay for the night in a modest hotel and take the bus for Ramgarh next morning.

David and Kim went to a modest hotel in front of the Nagpur Railway Station. They got a room and went there. After settling down, they decided to come on the balcony to watch the beautiful sunset.

As David and Kim were standing on the balcony watching the sunset, they saw another couple standing in front of the room next to their own. Both the couples felt like talking to each other. Hence they came closer.

David and Kim were glad to learn that the other couple, Gopal and Mira, was also going to Ramgarh next morning. When David asked them why, Gopal revealed the story.

Gopal and Mira were a Hindu couple from Jodhpur

(Rajasthan). Rajasthan is a border state of India in the West beyond which there is the Thar desert and Pakistan. Gopal was a self-employed person, a lawyer. Gopal and Mira had average heights, average bodies (neither stout nor thin), the color of their skin was brown (due to the climate in that region), and they were neither rich nor poor- one could say, well to do. Gopal said that he and his wife had gone on a pilgrimage to Dwarka

(located on the shores of the Arabian Sea in the Saurashtra area of Western Gujarat). After they had performed their prayers, they saw a Sanyasi (an Ascetic) sitting with closed eyes near the main temple.

Grandpa's Stories about India

Gopal and Mira touched his feet as a mark of their respect for him. The Sanyasi opened his eyes and asked them what did they want. Frankly they said that they wanted more money. Gopal and Mira did not tell David and Kim that they had also asked the Sanyasi that they wanted family peace – something which they were not able to get in spite of all efforts. Then Gopal said that the Sanyasi gave them a Mantra (an aphorism) and said "Nagpur. Ramgarh. Umaria. Golden Hill. Go" and then went somewhere; in spite of much efforts they could not see him again. Since they were on a sightseeing and pilgrimage tour already, they decided to follow the instructions. They were actually planning to go to Ramgarh and from there to Umaria Village and then to the Golden Hill.

David and Kim could not believe. Then they narrated their own story. All started wondering if some heavenly power was guiding their movements for something good. Both the couples were happy to have company on way when moving in an entirely unknown area. Promising to meet next morning, both the couples went to bed.

Next morning David and Kim along with Gopal and Mira left Nagpur for Ramgarh by bus. As compared with train, the bus takes much more time. Then, buses to rather small towns go still slower. The 143 mile long journey took about six hours. At last they reached the small town of Ramgarh.

However when the two couples reached Ramgarh and started looking for some place to stay, they met another couple – a Sikh man with a wife. They were also trying to find a place to stay for the night. Talking to each other they came to know that the man was Khushwant and his wife was Gurmeet. Soon they found a small hotel and all decided to stay there. The three couples hired three rooms and settled down.

It was already evening. So they sat on the table for dinner. Talking to each other they found that next morning Khushwant and Gurmeet wanted to go to Umaria village, which was about 36 miles in the northwest of Ramgarh. David and Kim as well as Gopal and Mira felt bewildered to hear this. Yet suppressing their great curiosity, they asked Khushwant and Gurmeet the purpose of their visit. Khushwant told the story.

Khushwant said that they had come from Ferozepur on the northwestern border of Punjab beyond which there is Pakistan. They had a small factory of their own where they made some machine parts. Khushwant and Gurmeet both were tall, had average bodies, and were very fair (due to the cold climate in that area). They could be called rich compared with others. They had no child. Khushwant said that he and his wife had gone for pilgrimage to the Sikh shrine of Hemkunt Saheb in the Garhwal Hills in the Himalayas. After offering their prayers, they were returning. Near the temple gate, they met a strange man; he was unkempt, had long dirty hairs, a long dirty beard, had a necklace of some bones, and looked mad. He asked them if they had any wish in life. Khushwant and Gurmeet hardly wanted to talk to him. But compelled by their desire to have a child, they told him that all that they wanted was a child. The man gave them a slip of paper and ran away fast to the north of the temple. When the couple saw the slip, it contained these words" Nagpur. Ramgarh. Umaria. Golden Hill. Go". Khushwant and Gurmeet thought that it was some bad and cruel joke. But God had blessed them with everything except a child. So they decided to take a chance. And here they were on way to Umaria and Golden Hill.

When Khushwant and Gurmeet were narrating their story, David and Kim as well as Gopal and Mira were listening with rapt attention. Their curiosity and excitement was mounting with every word that was being said. When the story was complete, the listeners narrated their stories to the Sikh couple. Now they were three couples together on way to Umaria village and Golden Hill, three miles away from there. It was decided to go to Umaria next morning. So everyone went to bed.

Next morning the three couples decided to go to Umaria. Hence, they went to the local Bus Stand. They learnt that there was no bus service direct to the Umaria village but the buses did pass from near the village. The three couples particularly the ladies felt that it would be so inconvenient to walk all that distance more so in the hot Sun. Hence, sort of an informal meeting of the three couples started as to what should be done. Hearing all this a man standing nearby came forward and asked them where did they want to go. The couples said that they wanted to go to Umaria and it was not certain how long they shall stay there – a few hours or even a day or two. The man suggested that the best for them was to hire a mini bus with a seating capacity of about 12 people. The man also pointed out towards the shop where such mini buses were available. The three couples went to the shop.

Grandpa's Stories about India

When the three couples were discussing their plans with the owner of the shop, another couple standing nearby came forward. The man said that they also wanted to go to Umaria, that they were not getting any transport, and that sharing the mini bus would be cheaper for everyone. The idea clicked. There was, however, another problem. There was no driver available. But Khushwant said that he was very good at driving and the last man – Mohammad – said that he was a very good mechanic. The mini bus was hired immediately. The four couples immediately left for Umaria.

While driving to Umaria, the three couples asked Mohammad to introduce himself. Mohammad said that he was a Muslim gentleman from Trivandrum, which is located on the southernmost end of India. With him was his wife Yasmin. Mohammad and Yasmin were of dark complexion (since it is so hot in south almost throughout the year), they were of average height, but had rather heavy bodies. Mohammad was a government employee and they were rather poor. When the three couples asked Mohammad to tell the purpose of their visit to Umaria, Mohammad revealed the mystery.

One night when Mohammad and his wife were sleeping, Yasmin saw a dream. In her dream, she saw an old gentleman with a long white beard and long white hairs. He was wearing a white robe from neck to ankles. He was smelling Henna. He said that God was pleased with them and they could ask for anything they wanted. Yasmin said that they only wanted God's blessings. The old man told her to go with Mohammad to Nagpur – Ramgarh – Umaria – Golden Hill and offer their prayers sincerely. Then the old man vanished and Yasmin woke up. When Yasmin told the dream to Mohammad, he said that he had also seen the old man in his dream but could not remember the rest. So next morning, Mohammad and Yasmin decided to go to the chief priest in the mosque. When they narrated the contents of their dream, the old chief priest said that since they had been told to go somewhere to offer prayers to God, they should go there. However, being rather poor, Mohammad and Yasmin had no money to undertake the journey. The chief priest arranged the same. That is how they could come to this place.

As Mohammad and Yasmin narrated their story, the remaining three couples listened carefully in silence. Then they revealed their stories. Now it was clear and certain that some heavenly power had brought the four couples together for some good. Thus they arrived in Village Umaria.

Umaria was a small village with a few huts here and there and a few small shops located mostly in the huts where people lived. Since Khushwant was driving the mini bus, he asked a local man the route to go to the Golden Hill. The man looked at him in great confusion but then told him to go three miles toward north. The mini bus moved accordingly.

Within a few minutes, they reached what was called the Golden Hill. Actually it was a huge leveled ground of the size of a football field. In the middle of the ground, there was a hillock. The four couples decided to climb the hillock. Reaching the top, they found that there were four beautiful trees in a circular form not very far from each other yet separate and in the middle of the trees, there was a cool area duly shaded by the surrounding trees. There was nothing else. And there was nobody else. All were confused. They could not decide as to what to do.

Then it was decided to have a little rest. As they were resting, they also discussed the big question – What to do? By this time it had become clear to all of them that they all had been brought here by God's will. Hence, they decided to pray God first.

The four couples offered their prayers in silence so as not to disturb each other. Then they started talking again. Someone said that the only thing they could do was to dig. But they had no tools to do that. Khushwant went to the Umaria village and returned with some tools. Then holding each other's hand , they formed the biggest possible human circle. They divided the small area into four parts and started digging from four sides.

Not used to digging and manual work, the digging was slow. Then they got tired. They decided to rest for a while. They ate the food they had brought from Ramgarh. Then they rested a little again. Someone suggested to return. But someone suggested to dig a little more. There was confusion and disagreement. But at last, everyone agreed to work for about two hours more and if even then there was nothing, then to return to Ramgarh.

Two hours had just passed and, digging from four sides, they had come to almost one point in the center. They were about to stop and leave. Suddenly someone said "Wait". Everyone stopped. The man said that he had felt something hard inside and there was also a sound

, perhaps, of metal. Everyone got excited. They forgot the time limit they had set. They started digging with renewed vigor. Digging a little more, they could now see a metal jar.

Before the jar could be taken out, somebody asked as to what should be done with the jar and its contents if any. They all agreed that the contents of the jar, whatever they are, shall be distributed equally among the four couples.

The jar came out. It was opened. The diamonds and jewels inside started glittering in the daylight of the Sun. Everybody was so happy. Feeling encouraged by their success, they did more digging. Gradually, three more jars came out making a total of four jars, all containing the same thing – diamonds and valuable jewels.

They decided to thank God first of all which they did in their hearts silently. Then contents of each jar were divided equally into four parts, one for each couple. Then they decided to leave. However, before leaving they also decided to do two things. First, they decided that nobody shall speak a word about what God had blessed them with. Second, they decided that they shall not return to the places they had come from but shall settle down in Ramgarh and establish their own enterprises for production of goods needed by the people; behaving like trustees, they shall take only minimum money from the enterprise, and reinvest the remaining money to expand and develop it further.

Then they returned to Ramgarh. Soon the four couples bought land in Ramgarh. They constructed their residential houses and factory buildings. In the meantime, they also called their families. Then they started living happily.

One day, Gurmeet was sick. She went to the Doctor. She was told that she was going to have a baby. David and Kim became so busy with their work that Kim totally forgot her serious disease – it was only stomach ulcers caused by severe depression ; soon it was cured with the help of medicines. Gopal and Mira never forgot the Mantra given to them by the Sanyasi in Dwarka – "Lead a simple life. Never think about what others are not doing to make you happy but always think about how and what you can do to make others , particularly those whom you love, happier"; they never had any problem thereafter. Their poverty gone, Mohammad and Yasmin also became happy.

Ram M. Saxena

This is an *entirely imaginary* story – *totally untrue*. But *totally true* is the message it gives.

A family or a community or a nation or the whole World can achieve peace, affluence, and happiness only when men and women from all places, and of all races, religions, castes, classes, colors, appearances, professions, and so on shed their mutual differences and prejudices and work together with full concentration using whatever skills and abilities God has blessed them with. This is so because let us remember - *United We Stand.*

THE CHRISTMAS CAKE

NOTE : True

A large number of events occur in the life of all of us. However, we tend to forget most of them. Particularly the events of our childhood get erased by the subsequent events of our adolescence, youth, late youth and old age. Years start coming together. And at times we even start wondering if we were ever children. This is rather unfortunate because childhood is the most pleasant and wonderful part in the life of a person. It is to be enjoyed forever - on a real time basis as a child during childhood, and later by sometimes recalling the memories of childhood, which not only refreshes our bored personality but also rejuvenates us.

But let me not write an essay on childhood; who wants to read these days and, moreover, who cares to read something serious. So let me return to my main task i.e. my story of the Christmas Cake.

This happened about fifty-five years ago. Then I was about five years old. I distinctly remember it was the period of winters, and since the story is about the Christmas Cake, it must have been the month of December, a little closer to the great festival.

At that time, my father was a Professor of Commerce at the renowned University of Lucknow. We used to live in a rented house with three floors near the City Railway Station in Lucknow. On the bottom floor, my father had his study room and a visitors' room, my mother had her kitchen and pantry, my two elder sisters had their reading room, my two elder brothers had their reading room, and there was a small courtyard, restroom, etc.

Then, on the middle floor, there were bedrooms. There was a big bedroom in which my father had his bed, my mother had her bed, I had my bed, and there was a Baby Cot (Crib) in which my younger brother used to sleep. Attached to the bedroom were two box rooms, one for my father and the other for my mother. Then there was a small courtyard. Beyond that there was a bedroom with two huge beds, one for my two brothers and the other for my two sisters. There were restrooms adjacent to the bedroom.

Then there was the top floor. It had only one room. It was for my eldest sister who used to keep it so clean that whenever I used to go there, I used to love to roll on her bed for a while (of course, with my sister's permission; I am not amazed that my son had the same taste when he was a little child, and I am rather pleased to see that my thirteen month old grandson Dave has the same liking). By telling you the design of the house, I am not trying to expand the story or bore you with unnecessary details. The purpose is to familiarize you with the exact location of the arena where the Cake battle was fought.

So let's get back to the Cake story. I am sure it was a Sunday because on all other days all my brothers and sisters used to go to the Schools and my father to the University leaving my younger brother and I with my mother. On that day everyone was at home. As usual I had eaten my meals at about 11 AM and I was simply amusing myself with this and that in my bedroom.

At about 11:30 AM, my father came up to the bedroom along with a small box of about 6" x 6". It was beautifully packed. He gave it to my mother. I was most curious to know what it contained. My mother opened it. It contained a small Christmas Cake. I was so thrilled to see it. As mothers know their children too well, before I could ask her, she assured me that the Cake shall be cut at the afternoon Tea time i.e. at about 4.30 p.m. My heart sank with disappointment. Such a beautiful Cake and such a long waiting period. But I could do nothing. I was so little and everyone else was so big. I had no option, but to accept the discipline imposed by them.

My mother placed the Cake on the table kept in between the two big beds near the wall. I could not resist the temptation of taking a good look at it. Oh! What a beauty! What a design! What a wonderful color combination! How beautiful were the green leaves! And how lovely were the two pink flowers! The light green icing on the rest of the cake looked so inviting. Before water could start flowing out of my mouth, mother reminded me – Tea time.

With a heavy heart I went to my bed. But with a Cake so wonderful, so near, how could I fall asleep.

Everyone else had taken meals and gone to his/her room. My parents also took their meals. Then my father went to his study room to work. My mother went to her bed with my younger brother. Soon she slept, having spent a tiring and busy morning.

But I was wide-awake. I was restless. My heart said that there was no harm in taking another look – *only* a look – at the Cake. I got up and went to the table. It was there, smiling at me or at least so did it appear to me. I returned to my bed.

I had a very keen desire to taste the Cake but I had not forgotten my mother's words. I did not want to be known as a bad boy. But sleep was far away. Then I kept fighting with myself. *Eventually the Cake won.*

I got up and went to the table. Since the Cake was meant for everyone, I decided to taste just one leaf. The moment one leaf touched my tongue, it started demanding company. I had to yield to the demand. Being a rather kind-hearted person, I was more than generous in responding to the demand of the tongue. All the leaves on the Cake disappeared. I returned to my bed. But that was not the end.

I started wondering how would the tree on the Cake look with only two flowers and no leaves. So I got up again. One flower was taken away. Then the other flower vanished. I came to my bed.

I tried to sleep. But more was to come. It struck my mind that now on the light green icing on the Cake, there were only a few green branches; no leaves, no flowers. How awkward. Certainly it would look more aesthetic if the barren branches were also removed and there was left a clean ground. I took pains to do that. Mission, thus, accomplished to my satisfaction, I returned to my bed. But, before that I looked at my mother; she was fast asleep. Then I too fell asleep.

It must have been around 3.30 p.m. I was still deep in my sleep enjoying my childhood dreams, with Cake leaves and flowers in my stomach, when it appeared to me as if some one was pulling me by my ear. Even in my dream, I could not believe this because I knew that I was dear to everyone in the family. But soon it appeared that the pull of the reality was stronger than the pleasure of the dreams. I got up and sat on my bed.

Hardly had I sat up when a slap landed on my head. That helped to transcend me fully from dream to reality. Now I was awake. I opened my eyes and saw my eldest sister standing near my bed. She seemed to be angry.

Actually my eldest sister was senior to me by thirteen years. She used to take a lot of care of me. I used to love her a lot. And hence I also used to be afraid of her. How could I afford to see her angry? When I saw her angry, I felt that something had gone wrong somewhere. I also felt that probably it had something to do with me. And perhaps it was the Cake.

Before I could say anything, my sister shouted at me "You fool. Why did you spoil the Cake"? What could I say? Did I do anything? Certainly not. *It was the Cake, which did everything.* The Cake was so attractive and I was so little to resist the temptation. However, my mother came to my rescue and the matter almost ended there.

For a long time, I was not very clear about the wrong I had done. It was only after a long time that I realized my mistake. The Christmas Cake was for everyone and not for me alone. I should have waited. Further, I should not have done anything like a thief.

But one thing I shall admit in all sincerity and seriousness. It has been about fifty-five years since then. But, still if I see a Christmas Cake, I am reminded of that Cake. It was really delicious.

TEARS OF LOVE

NOTE : True

When Mumtaz Mahal, the beloved wife of the famous King Shah – É – Jahan was on the death bed, the King asked her lovingly if she wanted him to do anything for her even after her death. The Queen asked the King to build an exquisite mausoleum in her memory after her death. The mausoleum that King Shah – É – Jahan built is the Taj Mahal known as the Seventh Wonder of the World. One author has described it as the "Tear of Love on the Cheek of Beauty". This story is neither about Shah – É – Jahan, nor about Mumtaz Mahal, nor even about the Taj Mahal. Far from that, it is about the "Tears of Love on the Cheeks of Duty".

As far as I remember it was October 1971. At that time I was a Lecturer in Commerce in the University of Jodhpur (Rajasthan). Because of the prevailing conditions, it was a rather heavy and demanding assignment. I used to give twenty-one lectures on four different courses every week to under-graduate and graduate students. That needed a lot of preparation at home. The Faculty of Commerce used to work in the morning i.e. from 7.30 a.m. to 12.45 p.m. Whenever we had special lectures, seminars, etc, we used to meet again in the afternoon at 4 p.m. and it mostly lasted two to three hours. In addition, I used to give one lecture in the evening also to make a little more money.

Besides teaching in the University, I had my own independent research work and at that time, my book writing work was in full speed. Moreover, candidates appearing at the various examinations of the Indian Institute of Bankers used to hold special lectures twice a year where I was invariably invited to teach; of course I used to get a small payment for that too.

In short, at that time I was too busy with my professional work. On the family side, we had a little son of five years whom we called Sumeet and a daughter of about twenty-two months whom we called Seema. This story is particularly about my daughter Seema.

As said earlier, I used to be extremely busy with my professional responsibilities. My wife Mona used to look after the kids most affectionately and manage the domestic affairs in a most brilliant way. Of course, I used to help her wherever I could specially with grocery.

In spite of my extreme pre-occupation with my professional and family responsibilities, I used to some how find some time every day to be with my son and daughter .Every day after the dinner, I used to take little Seema in my arms and go for a short walk say of about half a mile in the neighborhood. Mostly while going, we talked about the most wonderful things in the world i.e. she would tell me the few words she had learnt, I would tell her how much I loved her, she would kiss me sometimes, and I would pat her gently on the back and with my rough and tired fingers

(fingers tired with long hours of writing – there was no Computer at that time) comb her beautiful thick hairs. All this and the cool comforting breeze of the desert evening was mostly enough to put dear Seema to sleep. Then, I used to return home and put her in the little crib beside our double bed.

This was the routine I used to maintain daily . Sometimes there was a slight change in the timing, but the contents remained the same. But then one day, there was a lapse. This is the story of that serious lapse and that day.

It so happened that I had almost completed my day. I had worked in the University and in the evening delivered two lecturer in the Indian Institute of Bankers. If I remember correctly, I was also not feeling too well. I was almost totally exhausted. We took our dinner. Then , being totally tired , we decided to go to bed. But that was the blunder.

As soon as the lights were put out and we started to go to bed, little Seema started crying. Since I was rather unwell, my wife Mona tried to handle the case of dear Seema. But Seema continued to cry. Mona knew that I was unwell So she did her best to pacify the little child. But Seema would not respond.

Though I was lying on the bed, I was not asleep. I was also wondering what the matter was. There is a saying that men think that they know but the women know better. That must have been the case. This is so because at last Mona could somehow understand what the matter was. Since a lady can understand another lady better, Mona had probably understood little Seema.

Mona told me that little Seema was angry . I was surprised to hear that. I asked her why and what about. She told me that Seema was angry with me. Now that was more surprising.. Since at that time I was working on some serious macro-economic problem of the Indian economy, my understanding at the micro level had perhaps become too poor. I asked Mona why little Seema was angry with me. After some hesitation (hesitation was due to the fact that I was unwell and she did not want to bother me by telling the truth !), Mona told me the truth.

Mona told me that every day in the evening I had been taking dear Seema in my arms and going out for a little walk before she (and we) eventually slept but on that day, I had not honored the daily routine. I was surprised to hear that. And immediately I realized my mistake. Duty first, and duty last.

Late in the evening in October it gets a little cold in Jodhpur and more so for a little child of twenty-two months. I requested Mona to give me some medicine for headache , which she did very happily, being so fond of treating patients though without any formal knowledge of the subject (believe me, she is also very good at it, at least, for me). Then I decided to go out.

I wrapped little Seema in a light woolen shawl , took her in my arms, and went out - for our wonderful daily routine of exclusive father – daughter walk. But Seema was still angry and she was still crying though certainly not as loudly as she was doing before. She was very intelligent and smart even at that age; she had guessed that what she wanted was coming.

As I walked on the lonely street, little Seema's cries gradually mellowed ; but they were still there. Tears were still coming from out of her otherwise twinkling eyes and rolling down her little sweet cheeks . To make her protest and anger clear and complete, Seema was wiping her tears with her little palm and fingers and then to make sure that I understood her emotion, she was smearing my face with her tears. Overwhelmed by the emotions a few tears also came from out of my eyes.

I did my best to pacify Seema. A sweet little child, she immediately understood my feelings and slept in my arms as usual – blessed is a child's heart that is easily pleased. I returned home and placed her in the crib. Seema slept. And so did we.

Today Seema is a Physician in Phoenix and lives nearby. As I record this story, she is expected any moment to pick up her twenty-seven month old son Krsna; right now Mona is amusing Krsna with "Old McDonald had a farm……..".

Even today, sometimes, when I look at Seema, I am reminded of her tears on my cheeks. How true was Byron, when he said "The drying up a single tear has more of honest fame than shedding seas of gore". It was a heavenly bliss. I miss my little sweetie pie so much. But Krsna compensates it rather well.

Children like to have a routine. Those who take care of them should try to honor that as best as possible. And children know how to communicate effectively, their anger and their love. One should never under-estimate the smartness and brilliance of the little angels.

Grandpa's Stories about India

SPEAK THE TRUTH (?)

He was a young kid. His name was Ram. He was about five years old. He had started understanding something of the World.. It was Summer vacation in his School. Hence, he was at home. When kids of this age are at home due to a vacation in the School, it becomes very difficult to engage them constructively. The task becomes more difficult if it is summer when during the daytime it is so hot outside in the open that children simply cannot be allowed to play there lest they get a heat stroke. However, Ram was a good boy. He was playing with his toys

After sometime, Ram felt a little bored. So he went to his mother who was working in the kitchen. When the mother asked what the matter was, Ram replied that he did not know what to do. Since it was already about noontime, the mother said "Let me complete my work. Then I shall take my lunch. And then I shall tell you a story".

This sounded too good to Ram. .He still used to love to lye down with her mother and listen to the wonderful stories his mother narrated. It seemed to him that his mother knew all the wonderful stories of the World and she had with her an unending stock of stories. So he awaited the moment with the excitement of a child.

About forty-five minutes passed. Mother had completed her daily chores. She went to her bedroom. Ram was already there. She stretched herself on the bed. Ram lay beside her.

Mother asked Ram which story did he want to listen. Ram said that just any story was welcome as long as it was good . Mother said that instead of any one story , she shall narrate several anecdotes – one anecdote daily - and then see if they could put them together and learn anything from out of it.

(1)

Mother narrated this anecdote. Once there was a boy. His name was Ashok. He used to live with his parents and elder sister. He was very fond of candies as most kids are. One day, the candy man came with his stock of candies . The boy wanted to buy a candy. But he did not have any money. He had already spent his pocket money. His craving for candy was so strong that he quietly stole some money from his father's wallet. Since the money stolen was very small, no one could find out. But the mother saw the boy eating candy. She asked him how he bought the candy. The boy told a lie. He said that he had saved some money in the past and he had used the same.

Then, mother asked Ram if the boy had done a right thing. Too young to analyze and interpret, Ram kept silent. His mother said that the boy had done a very bad thing. He had stolen which is a bad thing because we should never steal anything from anybody. Then, he had lied to his mother, which was again a bad thing to do because we should always speak the truth. .

By the time mother completed the anecdote, she found that Ram was about to sleep. She stopped and slept herself.

(2)

Next day, Ram's mother narrated this anecdote. Once there was a boy. His name was Shyam. He used to live with his parents. One day, Shyam was playing in the family room at home. While so doing , he tossed his ball up in the air and tried to catch it. However, he missed the ball. The ball instead fell on the ground, then bumped up and collided with a teacup on the table. The cup fell down and broke down. Shyam collected the pieces and threw them in the trash. Since there were many cups in the house, nobody could know about it. After several days, Shyam's mother asked him if he had seen that particular cup. Shyam thought that if he tells the truth, he may be penalized. So he told a lie and said that he did not know anything in the matter.

Then Ram's mother asked him if Shyam had done a right thing. The boy kept quiet. His mother said that Shyam had done a wrong thing by playing ball in the family room where accidents could happen. Then he had done a wrong by trying to conceal the matter by hiding the broken pieces. We should assume responsibility for what we do. He had also done a bad thing by telling a lie to his mother because we should always speak the truth.

By the time mother completed the anecdote, she found that Ram was about to sleep. She stopped and slept herself.

(3)

Next day Ram's mother narrated this anecdote. Once there was a boy. His name was Gopal. He used to live with his parents. One-day Gopal's mother gave him milk to drink. Gopal did not like drinking milk. He used to drink milk only under pressure from his mother. He took the glass of milk to the patio and threw the milk outside on the lawn below. When his mother asked him if he had taken the milk, Gopal said that he had. After a little while, when his mother went on the patio, she slipped on the creamy milk and got a little hurt. She told Gopal not to lie in future but always speak the truth.

Since Ram was about to sleep, his mother stopped and slept herself.

(4)

Next day Ram's mother narrated this anecdote. Once there was a boy. His name was Raj. He lived with his parents. One night everybody was sleeping. Late in the night, there was some loud sound of something falling on the ground. Raj's father got up. He woke up Raj's mother. Then he told her that probably thieves had entered the house. Just when Raj's mother was about to say something, two people entered the room. They had revolvers in their hands. One of them asked Raj's parents in a threatening tone "Where is the cash and jewelry"? Raj's mother kept silent. His father said "There is no jewelry in the house". But immediately Raj said

"No, father. We have jewelry in mother's box". The thieves were so happy. They took all the jewelry and cash from the box of Raj's mother. Then warning everyone to keep quiet, they escaped in the dark of the night.

Raj's parents were very angry. Raj asked them what wrong had he done. His father said "You should not have told the truth".

Since Ram was about to sleep, his mother stopped and slept herself.

(5)

Next day Ram's mother narrated this anecdote. Once there was a boy. His name was Deepak. He lived with his parents. One day his parents were fighting with each other about some family matter. Soon Deepak's mother started crying In the meantime, some guests came to their home. Deepak's father received the guests in the formal guest room. Not finding Deepak's mother there, one of the guests asked "Where is Deepak's mother "? Deepak's father said that she was a little busy in the kitchen and would come soon. But Deepak said "No,

Uncle. Father and mother were fighting. So mother is weeping in the bed room".

After the guests left, Deepak's parents were very angry. Deepak asked them what wrong had he done. His mother said "You should not have told the truth".

Since Ram was about to sleep, his mother stopped and slept herself.

(6)

Next day Ram's mother narrated this anecdote. Once there was a boy. His name was Shankar. He lived with his parents. One day, the neighbors sent some food to them. The food was tasted at the lunchtime. However, the parents did not like the food at all. Not only this, they threw the food in the trash. In the evening, Shankar went out to play with other kids in the neighborhood. Per chance he met the neighbors who had sent the food. They asked him if he liked the food they had sent. Shankar said

"I could d not even taste the food. My parents threw it in the trash". Naturally they felt hurt and told Shankar's parents as such.

Shankar's parents were very angry. They said "You should not have told the truth".

Since Ram was about to sleep, his mother stopped and slept herself.

(7)

Next day when Ram and his mother went to bed after their lunch, Ram's mother asked him "I told you six anecdotes during the last six days. Can you tell me what you have understood from them" ? Ram said that sometimes the boys were asked to speak the truth and then sometimes they were told not to speak the truth; therefore, Ram was confused as to what one should do.

Ram's mother said "Yes. I had thought that you may say something like this. Now listen carefully. One should always speak the truth. Even if one has done something wrong, he should tell the truth and assume responsibility for his action. Even if there is punishment for doing something wrong, one should accept it and make a determination not to repeat the wrong in future. As said by George Washington, the first President of the U S A, we all commit mistakes; but it is only the great who admit them and do not repeat them".

Ram's mother added "However, there are situations when one should not speak the truth. If there is no need to speak, one should not speak at all. Unless one is asked specifically to speak, one should not speak. If by speaking the truth, there is likely to be some loss or harm or someone is likely to feel displeased or hurt, one should not speak the truth".

Ram's mother added further "Yes. Then there are situations when one must speak and speak the truth. If by speaking the truth, you think someone shall feel pleased , do not hesitate to speak the truth. If , for example , you like the dress of someone, say so. If you like the food anywhere, say so. Particularly about the food or some other gift offered to you by somebody, never forget to thank and appreciate even if you do not like it. This is so because more than the food or the gift given to you, you appreciate the sentiment of the other person who has done something for you so affectionately. If you like someone's lawn or garden or home, just say so".

Then Ram's mother said "In short, remember this mantra (aphorism) in Sanskrit language SATYAM BRUYAT, PRIYAM BRUYAT, NA BRUYAT SATYAM APRIYAM which means SPEAK THE TRUTH, SPEAK THE PLEASANT, DO NOT SPEAK THE UNPLEASANT TRUTH".

Ram M. Saxena

THE ICE CREAM MAN

NOTE : Based on true events narrated to me in 1957 by my friend Mahaveer who later died in his twenties

Bareilly is one of the most beautiful and lovable towns of India located in the Indo – Gangetic plains halfway between Lucknow and Delhi as a Gateway to the hills of Central Himalayas. About 80 miles southwest of Bareilly, located in the most fertile land in between the two holy rivers Ganga and Yamuna, is the small town of Kasganj.

There lived a man in Kasganj. Nobody knew his real name. However, everybody used to call him Munna. Actually the word Munna means a little cute boy. When he was born, his parents, out of their enormous love for the newborn , started calling him Munna. Their love continued irrespective of the age of the boy and naturally therefore the name Munna also continued. When relatives, friends, neighbors, and others heard the name Munna, they also started calling the boy by the same name. Though Munna had long ago crossed the stage of being a "Little Cute Boy"– now he was a grown up man with a wife and children , he was still Munna for everybody. Even he had reconciled with the situation.

Munna was an Ice Cream Hawker. He used to get up early in the morning everyday. He had four buffalos. He used to milk them early in the morning and his wife used to milk the buffalos in the afternoon. After milking the buffalos, Munna used to take out some milk for consumption of the family. He sold some to the neighbors. The remaining milk was put in the large Karahi (a saucer-shaped pan) on the Chulha (the earthen stove in which wood is used as fuel). Munna used to keep stirring the milk in the Karahi till after about two hours the extra water in the milk totally evaporated and what was left in the Karahi was something like a thick paste of milk. Then the Karahi was taken down the Chulha. The milk paste was allowed to cool down. After the milk paste had cooled down, Munna would add some fine granulated sugar, and a little of cardamom (Ilaichi) powder to it. Blending the whole thing together was tough and an art. Munna was so good at it. Now the Ice Cream material was ready.

Grandpa's Stories about India

Then Munna used to take his lunch and the short siesta. He was back at work around 1 p.m. Then, one by one he used to pick up the Ice – Cream Cones made of tin and fill the material carefully in the cones. The moment the cone was filled up, he would place a tin cap on it and part of the real genius lay in sealing the cap on the cone. The sealing was done with very thick paste of Maida

(Extremely fine wheat floor not containing any husk). The sealed cones were carefully placed, as they were ready one by one, in a large Matka (earthen pot like Mexican olla). The Matka used to contain not-too-small pieces of ice and salt. The Matka was kept in a corner of his workplace. By about 4 p.m. the yummiest Ice Cream in the whole world (and for the local people, the World meant Kasganj) was ready.

Then came the selling function. Munna used to lift the filled up Matka and keep it on his right shoulder; on his left shoulder he carried a small bag containing tree leaves of about 6" x 6" size for serving the Ice Cream. All this done, he could start his round of the market and residential area nearby.

The moment Munna started his round around 4.30 p.m., he used to announce loudly and in a melodious voice "Kulfi Malaiwali" (Rich Homemade Ice Cream). After every two – three minutes, the call had to be repeated because Munna was walking all the time and the set of people around was constantly changing.

The call was enough to change the course of events in the small town. Young in age and the young at heart all loved his Ice Cream. The moment they heard his call, their mouths used to get filled with water in anticipation of the most delicious Ice Cream they were about to eat. There were some who used to feel shy in admitting how much they loved the Ice Cream Munna sold. However, it was not a secret that sometimes they used to buy Munna's Ice Cream in the name of kids and devour it themselves quietly. Thus, all loved Munna's Ice Cream and hence all loved Munna. Naturally, Munna too loved all, particularly those who bought and appreciated his Ice Cream.

One day something sad happened. Lala Ghanshyam Das died. He was a rich man. Naturally his family and friends had to perform his last rites. The process was very streamlined and totally pre-determined under the Hindu religion. First of all a priest was called to perform the special prayers. Then the family and friends prepared a structure of totally new bamboos, resembling a scaffold. The dead body was placed on the scaffold and tied to it. Then it was decided to take his dead body to the cremation ground for burning.

The method of taking the corpse to the cremation ground also needs to be mentioned. It was considered to be an honor to the dead if the corpse was taken all the way to the cremation ground by his family and friends on their shoulders. Almost everybody knowing the dead used to be present and active on such an occasion of great importance, people kept changing shoulders, at will, every few steps. Bigger and richer the dead man, larger used to be the number of persons joining his funeral procession. People participated actively in such processions also because they knew that some day they too shall die and need some people to carry their own dead body.

Lala Ghanshyam Das was an important man and a rich man. So a large number of persons joined the funeral procession. Munna had known Lala Ghanshyam Das for a long time. Actually in his early life, Lala Ghanshyam Das was not so rich. In those days, he and Munna used to be very friendly and played together as little boys. Not only this, Lala Ghanshyam Das loved and appreciated Munna's Ice Cream. So Munna also joined the funeral procession.

Lala Ghanshyam Das had died around 2 in the afternoon. Hence by about 4 PM, all the needed formalities were completed at home and the funeral procession started for the cremation ground.

People who were closely related to the dead and those who were rich shouldered the corpse first. But they soon left it having done their social duty. The funeral procession was passing through the main market. Now Munna shouldered the corpse of Lala Ghanshyam Das along with some others.

So Munna was carrying the dead body of Lala Ghanshyam Das on his right shoulder. As he was doing this, he had also become emotional not only with the memory of the good old days with Lala Ghanshyam Das but also with the realization that Lala was such a lover of his Ice Cream.

Once the heavenly thought of his Ice Cream entered his mind, it wiped out all other earthly matters of lesser significance. He started thinking of the next day. He shall get up in the morning. Milk the buffalos. Prepare the Ice Cream. Keep it in the Matka. Place the Matka on his right shoulder. Start his walking and call out "Kulfi Malaiwali".

Munna had traveled only thus far in his dreamland. But some personality complexity created a bad situation. In reality also, everybody around heard the familiar voice "Kulfi Malaiwali".

Now, that was too much. Who likes such crude jokes on such serious occasions. Everybody present rebuked Munna for being so ill mannered and for showing such disrespect to the dead. It is said that one should not show disrespect to the dead even if he had been a bad man. And Lala Ghanshyam Das was really a good man. Moreover he was also a good friend of Munna. So Munna's behavior was found to be totally unacceptable and condemnable.

Munna too felt sad, bad, and ashamed. He never wanted to do that. But sometimes we speak what we really WANT to speak and not what we SHOULD speak; it is said that when the sub-conscious dominates the conscious then this happens. Perhaps the same thing happened with Munna on that occasion. Perhaps this happened because Munna had identified himself too closely with his work . I think even if Munna had been given a fortune, he would still have loved to make and sell his Ice Cream. How much he loved to do it and how proud he was of his work. Whatever may have been the psychological reason, Munna had to cut a sorry figure.

The story tells us that when we do something, we should concentrate all our attention on THAT WORK and THAT WORK ALONE till it is completed. This is so because if in the meantime we start thinking about any other matter or matters then at least in our mind, we CAN become confused. That confusion can ruin our work or paralyze our action or create ugly situations like the one Munna had to face.

True, one who tries to be everywhere, gets nowhere. No one can ride two horses or sail in two boats simultaneously. Work with concentration brings success in life.

Ram M. Saxena

THE HINDU TEMPLE

NOTE : Basic event is true and was narrated to me by my wife Mona who hails *from Bareilly*

When India was about to regain its freedom from the British rule on August 15, 1947, Mr. Mohammad Ali Jinnah , the chief leader of the Muslim League had said that if a separate Nation (Pakistan) was not created for Muslims, then the country (India) will have to face a civil war on communal lines. On the contrary, Mahatma Gandhi, the Father of the Nation , had said that India shall be divided into two nations on communal lines and a separate Nation of Pakistan shall be created "Only over my dead body".

The subsequent events are known to all. India was divided and Pakistan was created and so much more happened. The purpose here is not to perform a post – mortem examination of the horrifying events which involved, among other things, migration of population on a scale which was unprecedented in the history of the World; that has already been done innumerable times by innumerable experts with no tangible achievement. The purpose here is also not to say who was right or who was wrong. The silent majority was defeated and the vocal minority had its way.

However, one thing is clear. The partition of India was a decision of the politicians, by the politicians, and for the politicians . Neither Hindus nor Muslims wanted it. In spite of so many years since then, most people in both the countries – India and Pakistan – still feel sorry about the horrifying event which only brought them more of poverty and suffering . They had lived as friends and brothers for centuries and had no problem in continuing to live as such forever . Even after partition of India, a very large number of Muslims had decided to continue to stay in India , which was naturally their own country. Even today overwhelming majority of Hindus and Muslims live as friends and brothers in India. The present story is about one of the many such events, which bear testimony to that fact and feeling. (The purpose of this story is not to create a political stunt but to inform people about the true fraternal feelings among the two communities of India.).

Grandpa's Stories about India

Bareilly is one of the most beautiful cities of India. Located exactly mid-way between Lucknow, the former capital of the world renowned State of Avadh , and Delhi, the seat of the world famous Moghul Empire, Bareilly possesses an enviable blend of many things – the blend of Delhi Moghul culture and Lucknow Nawabi culture; the blend of Muslim culture of the Rohillas and Pathans (Bareilly is the heart of Rohilkhand) and Hindu culture of the local kings (the fort built by King Shobha Ram is still there in Bareilly); the blend of the Indian culture and the former British culture
(Bareilly was an important center of the British army and still there is British India Bazar in Bareilly Cantonment); the blend of agricultural and industrial cultures; and now the blend of tradition and modernity.

In that city of Bareilly, there lived a man. No one ever cared to find or ask him his formal name. He was known as Chinna Mian (the Tiny one) in his childhood. However, the name continued even beyond that wonderful stage of life.

Chinna Mian was a very poor man. The source of his livelihood was repair of the tin buckets , which people used for keeping water in their homes. He had a remarkable skill in replacing the bottoms of the leaking tin buckets. So naturally he was very popular. He lived in a dingy cell in a narrow lane (adjacent to Pheni Wali Gali) in Beharipur. That was his residence and workshop. The entrance door at his home was a torn curtain of jute cloth, which revealed his poverty more than it concealed the household.

Chinna Mian was a honest person. He was a religious person and had a very strong faith in God. He had a strong belief that God is the friend of those who have no other friend. He was a Muslim by religion. But that hardly made a difference in his popularity in cosmopolitan Bareilly. Though poor, he had a keen hidden wish to do something good and memorable .

God has unique ways of blessing His devotees. He knew the noble wish , which Chinna Mian had, in his heart. Hence , God found a way to bless Chinna Mian and give him an opportunity to fulfill his hidden wish.

Though Chinna Mian was poor, he used to buy lottery tickets, that is, whenever he could afford to do that. It looks strange. But even today most of the lottery tickets in India are bought specially by the poor and the not-rich. It seems Chinna Mian already knew that someday he is sure to win a lottery and all that he has to do in the meantime is keep trying. True, unless one tries, and keeps trying, how can he ever hope to win or be able to achieve any result.

Perhaps for Chinna Mian the DAY had come. One day, all of a sudden, he came to know that he had won a very huge amount of money in lottery.

The amount won in lottery was so huge that it created enormous tension. The tension was not in the mind of Chinna Mian . For he treated it as a gift from God which indeed it was. Moreover, he treated it as money given to him by God mainly to hold in trust for some specific good purpose. It created tension only in the minds of others.

Many crooks, rich and the not-so-rich, unanimously felt that the gift from God had been ill-delivered; it was meant for them but due to some last minute mistake by God's Dispatch Clerk, the money had reached Chinna Mian instead of reaching them. Naturally they started scheming to grab the money.

One merchant advised Chinna Mian to become a partner in the business, which the merchant was already doing; however, this could not be done because being a local man, Chinna Mian was aware of the merchant's notoriety. Then, a moneylender told Chinna Mian to deposit the money with the moneylender and receive interest every month at home without doing anything and be free from all worries. It was well known that the money lender – a very shrewd man – had, in the past , freed many from their money. There was the building contractor who said that he could build a real royal palace for Chinna Mian at a very low cost. Chinna Mian knew that the building contractor had one important life principle - never stand below the roofs and above the bridges, which were built by him. And the self-advertised big man of the movies advised Chinna Mian to become a movie financier and receive highest profit without doing anything.

Chinna Mian quietly listened to all these unsought advises and invitations. It seems poverty had shown him enough of the World. He was , however, very clear in his mind. Then, he decided to proceed according to his own priorities .Now that he had the money, he decided first of all to fulfill his own cherished wish of the lifetime. He decided to build a Hindu Temple.

The moment Chinna Mian made it known that he wanted to build a Hindu Temple, there was an enormous clamor. The vehement opposition came mainly from those crooks whose advises had been ignored by Chinna Mian. One Hindu opposed construction of a Hindu

Temple by a Muslim. And a Muslim called Chinna Mian an infidel because ignoring the fact that he was a Muslim he wanted to build a Hindu Temple. Then some Hindus declared that no upper caste Hindu shall go to the Temple if and when it was built because the Temple to be built was to be for all Hindus – lower caste, upper caste, and the so-called untouchables, all included; though much of change has occurred in India since then, these sentiments were not non-existent in early 1950s when this event happened.

But Chinna Mian was totally undisturbed. He had a firm faith in God and in good deeds. So in spite of all opposition, he proceeded quietly. Land was bought in Chahwai locality. One very honest and God-fearing building contractor was engaged. Some learned Hindu priests were requested to advise. And construction of the Hindu Temple started.

Once the construction started, there was no shortage of good people who came forward to help in all possible ways. Even the crooks started thinking that it would be a good business strategy to give up opposition and take advantage of the new opportunity for doing some business. Soon the entire clamor disappeared.

Since the construction planned was extremely beautiful and artistic, it took many years to be completed. But in a few years the most beautiful marble Hindu Temple with gold and silver decoration here and there was completed.

In due course, Chinna Mian went to heaven. But the Hindu Temple built by him is still there in Chahwai area of Bareilly. It contains idols of almost all the Hindu Gods and Goddesses. Any and every Hindu can freely go to offer prayers. The Hindu Temple stands not only for the Hindu religion. Perhaps more than that it stands as a symbol of communal harmony, which is a unique characteristic of India's culture.

The story tells us that if one wants to do something really good, even God helps him and if at all there is any opposition, then with God's grace, it disappears in no time. Hence, one should have a strong faith in God and in doing good.

Ram M. Saxena

THE RICH MAN AND THE SHOES

NOTE : The basic event on which the story is based, is true and was narrated to me by my wife Mona who hails from Bareilly

One dark and cold November evening, he was left as a newborn on the main door of the City Orphanage Bareilly. There he learnt to read and write. He also developed a keen interest in reading on all possible subjects and matters of life and death. At the age of ten he left the Orphanage to study in the University of real life.. For a week he washed utensils in a roadside restaurant. For two weeks he assisted in a food grain shop. For a month he worked as helper in a provision (grocery) store. For a year he worked as a helper in a general store. Then he spent two years in the shop of a cloth merchant. Thereafter he became a servant in the shop of Jagdish Seth , a Jeweler and a Moneylender.

Jagdish Seth was an experienced and intelligent man. He immediately found out that the boy was honest and hard working. Gradually the boy's work changed from cleaning the shop to receipt and delivery of money, bullion and ornaments. He also learnt melting of gold and silver and making of ornaments. By the time he was eighteen years, he had well learnt the work of a jeweler and a moneylender. With the support and guidance of Jagdish Seth, he started his own small business of Jeweler and Moneylender. Through sheer hard work, honesty, concentration, good behavior, and God's blessings, he became known as Dharam Seth.

By the time Dharam Seth was 40 years old, he had earned and saved a lot of money and built lots of assets. He had a big jewelry business, a well respected money-lending business, many houses, many plots of land , many shops, and much more. He heavily supported the City Orphanage, started two Schools, set up a charitable dispensary, and established a vocational school particularly for orphans and widows.

He had married Geeta an orphan girl. They also got a son Kuber. But due to some serious disease, Geeta could not bear more children. On the contrary, she became bed-ridden.

Dharam Seth and his wife Geeta were respected deeply and widely. Considering the excellent reputation of Dharam Seth and Geeta, Kamal Seth married his only motherless child Maya with Kuber.

But it is said that good people are needed everywhere including Heaven. Once Kamal Seth was going from Bareilly to Allahabad for a legal case in the High Court. His car met with an accident. He died in a moment on the spot. Perhaps this was not enough. So Dharam Seth also died soon of a heart attack.

At the age of 20 years, Kuber inherited the enormous wealth of his father and that of his father – in – law. Maya had no mother and Kuber's mother Geeta was bed-ridden. This made Kuber Seth free from all checks and controls with enormous wealth and the power that comes with it.

Since Kuber Seth had suddenly become owner of enormous wealth without doing anything at all from his side to earn it, he turned almost mad with pride, power, and freedom.

Kuber Seth was an extremely ill – behaved person; he was diametrically opposite to his late father. He had a strong conviction that anybody and everybody in the whole world could be manipulated and dominated by him with the money, which he had.

Since Kuber Seth was owner of a rather big business house, people used to invite him frequently for luncheons, dinners, parties, etc. Out of his vanity and obstinacy, he never attended those parties. He always thought that because of the money, which somehow he had , he was too big and too higher than all others in the world. Sometimes when he was invited he had nothing else to do but even then he preferred to sit idle at home or go somewhere else to waste his time rather than attend the social gathering. Kuber was idle because Maya managed the household under the overall guidance of Geeta from her bed and the trusted employees who had been appointed by the late Dharam Seth and Kamal Seth managed the business. In the absence of anyone at the top to supervise, however, the business had started dwindling.

Neither at home nor anywhere else Kuber Seth ever appreciated anybody doing anything good. He always thought that it was the duty of others to do things for him and it was not at all necessary for him to do anything for others or even to feel grateful. He took everybody and everything for granted.

But the worst has not yet been mentioned here. Kuber Seth was very fond of shoes. He had a very large number of shoes. He hardly knew how many pairs he had. He liked to wear a new pair of shoes every time he changed his dress, which probably was the only thing he did. When he used to feel bored with a pair of shoes, he simply threw it in a small room in a corner of the house. The small room had gathered a huge stock of old shoes.

In India there is a custom that whenever someone dies, then all those who were related to him or knew him in any capacity visit the house of the dead to express their condolences and moreover to carry the dead-body to the cremation ground as a mark of respect to the dead. People honor and follow this custom even to this day. This is so simply because someday all of us have to die and then we shall all need some people to take us to the cremation ground.

Kuber Seth was a true and glaring example of the related anecdote from the epic Mahabharata . Briefly, near the water pond in the garden of the Yaksha, the invisible voice asked "KIM ASHCHARYAM" ? (What is the greatest surprise ?). And Yudhishthira replied "Every day we see so many dying but it never occurs to us that someday we too shall die. If only we remember our death ,we shall refrain from so much evil". That was the perfect reply.

But Kuber Seth had managed to forget the greatest truth of life under the false intoxication of his wealth and power. He had become so proud and mad with his money and resultant power that he had adopted a very vulgar practice. Whenever someone died and he was informed, instead of going to the house of the dead himself, Kuber Seth used to send a pair of his old useless shoes to represent him. Apparently, in his estimation, other people were worth only one of the pairs of his old useless shoes.

Many people felt greatly offended by the crude and vulgar behavior of Kuber Seth. But then Kuber Seth had the money and the power – power , even to harm people if he decided to do so. Hence feeling greatly hurt, people kept quiet.

Time continued to move as it always does. Kuber Seth and Maya got two sons and a daughter. They married them early, which was the custom in such families in those days – around 1950s.

But then the DAY came soon. At the age of 45 years, Kuber Seth died. It was a very big event in the then rather small town of Bareilly. Hundreds of people came to know of the sad news.

But then a very strange thing happened. The dead body of Kuber Seth was lying in the front patio of the huge house. It was time to take the body to the cremation ground . But there was not even one person on the huge lawn in front of the patio. However, the lawn was filled with hundreds of pairs of shoes. These were the pairs of shoes sent by the people of Bareilly to reciprocate the behavior extended to them by Kuber Seth all his life.

Finding this too humiliating but only appropriate under the situation, the two sons decided to do something. Leaving the dead body at home, they started going from door to door to neighbors and others. The sons apologized for the behavior of their late father and promised that they shall be nice to everyone. Hardly had they visited a few houses when people pardoned the whole thing and came running for the needful. The funeral procession was huge. The last rites were performed in a most graceful manner – not as a mark of respect to the dead but as a mark of pardon for the living. Sons always behaved nicely – like their grandfather- and always got respect and help from everybody.

The people of Bareilly pardoned Kuber Seth . But history does not forgive anyone. It has been a very long time – several decades – since all this happened. But even today everyone in Bareilly knows this story. And sooner or later it is narrated to all those who come in contact with the people of Bareilly. The purpose is not to show disrespect to the dead but to admonish the living.

This story tells us that if a person gets enormous wealth without doing anything to earn it and that too at an early immature age, then it is most likely that he shall lose his mental balance. Once the mental balance is lost, the person is virtually ruined - QUOS DEUS VULT PERDERE PRIUS DEMENTAT, which means those whom god wishes to destroy, He first drives mad. One should do his best to maintain his sanity and pray God to bless him with wisdom.

Ram M. Saxena

BEING METHODICAL

Anand was a good boy. He was in his mid-teens. He was a High School student. His family included an elder sister and grandparents besides his parents. They all lived in a beautiful large house in a good neighborhood.

Anand was an ambitious boy. He wanted to become a physician and go very high up in his life. He also used to work hard for that. He was reasonably good at his studies. He was also a good football player. He was loved by the family at home and liked by the friends outside the home. However, at times, he used to get bumped.

Once it so happened that on Thursday Anand came to know that he shall have his Physics examination on Monday. Anand loved Physics and hence he was very good at it. Since he was very good at Physics, he was not worried about the examination. He thought of a last minute brush up on Sunday and he knew that it was enough for him to get a good grade. He utilized the intervening time for other activities he liked. Then came Sunday. Anand started looking for his Physics book. But he could not find it. Since he knew that the book was somewhere near, he was not much worried. But it could not be located. Now Anand started feeling a little worried. But still he was sure of finding the book soon. So he was still cool. Some more time passed. The book could not be found. Anand decided to take his lunch and then search the book afresh. The lunch was over. The search started again. Still no trace of the book. Anand got worried. As the day moved from noon to afternoon to evening, Anand's worry also heightened and turned into panic. By the time it was 7 p.m. Anand was almost mad. He could not trace the book he had. And he knew that he could not buy another copy because it was Sunday when all the bookshops were closed. He could not also borrow the book from any of his friends because on the eve of the examination, they needed the book themselves. Sunday turned into Monday. Anand had to take the Physics examination without studying at all. Though he took the examination, he got a poor grade and that too in Physics where he always got an A. Sure, it was a setback - a bummer. The book was later found under the bed on which Anand slept.

Grandpa's Stories about India

Then it was another day. Anand was a member of the School Football team. He played well. A team is able to do well only when all the members do their best. But Anand was rather too good. Hence the team greatly valued his presence and participation. The team had a match at 5 p.m. on Friday. Anand had been practicing well. Hence he knew he shall do well in the match. Then came the fateful Friday. Anand started searching his football boots to go to the match. But the boots were not there. He searched again. Still he could not find the boots. Some more time passed. But the boots could not be seen. The time for the match was fast approaching. The boots were not traceable. Anand's tension was mounting with every tick of the clock.. But nothing could be done. Increasing tension started distorting his rationality . He started looking at odd places. That only wasted his time all the more. But he had no success. At last he decided to go to the match without his own football boots. He decided to borrow the boots from someone in the School. When he reached, the match was just about to start. His substitute had already been chosen and was about to be called. Just then Anand arrived on the scene full of panic. His skill as a football player was well known and respected.. Though he was a little late, he was accommodated and allowed to play. But first he had to borrow someone else's football boots. The search and the begging started. Soon it was over. Anand got boots of Suresh. He put them on and entered the field. He tried to do his best. But could not succeed. Anand's feet were a little broader than that of Suresh. Hence the borrowed boots were a little too tight. That caused discomfort every time Anand tried to move. Though Anand's team won, Anand was warned about his below expectation performance. Later, the boots were found in the backyard at home.

Anand was feeling a little bored after serious studies for many days. And so were three of his best friends. They all decided to go to the new movie in the town. But there was a big rush because so many people wanted to see it. Tickets were not easily available . After some effort, tickets were bought for Saturday evening. It was planned that after the movie they shall all join for dinner in a restaurant. Then came the Saturday evening. Anand was all set to go out for the movie. He thought of carrying his ticket along. He looked here and there, right and left, below and above, in front and behind, inside and outside. But his movie ticket had disappeared or at least so did it seem then. Eventually, Anand decided to go to the movie theatre without the ticket. He went to the Theatre. But how could they allow someone without a ticket and that too in a movie where there was already a big rush of people with valid tickets. The movie started but Anand was still outside the hall. His friends waited for him for sometime but at last promised to meet in the restaurant for dinner and went inside the hall. Anand had a very bad time. He loitered here and there for the duration of the movie. Then, after that he went to the restaurant. Since he had reached early, he had to wait for sometime. At the proper time his friends came. They were all glad about the movie and they talked about it. But Anand was bored and sad. The dinner was over and everyone went home. After a week Anand found the ticket in one of his books.

Ramesh was one of his best friends. He was celebrating his Birthday by a big party. He had invited many naturally including Anand. The party was on a Friday evening. Then came the wonderful Friday evening. Anand had put on his best dress. He had carefully combed his hairs, which he loved very much. He went out of the house to ride his motorbike. Reaching the motorbike he found that he had left the keys in his room. He went back to his room. He knew that the keys shall be in a corner of his study table. But they were not there. He searched in a relaxed manner, then in a worried manner, and eventually in a state of frenzy. But the keys were not found. Finding no other alternative, Anand hired a taxi and went for the party. He attended the party but his excitement and happiness had already gone before the party due to the motorbike key tragedy. Two days later the keys were found below the refrigerator in the Kitchen

One day it so happened that while cooking food in the kitchen,. Anand's mother splattered the cooking oil in the cooking pan and sustained burns on her hands. The burns were not severe but certainly they hurt. Anand was studying in his room. Hearing the commotion he too rushed to the kitchen. He was much pained to see what had happened. But he knew that there was excellent medicine for burns in the house and if applied immediately it not only provided comfort but also fast cure. Anand looked for the medicine tube in the medicine chest. He did not find it there. Suddenly it struck his mind that he had taken the medicine tube to his room for applying it on his small burn on the left hand. He dashed to his room .He searched the medicine tube everywhere but could not find it. In the end, it was decided to give up the search and buy another tube immediately. As this was

Grandpa's Stories about India

going on, Anand's grandfather entered the room with a new tube of medicine; he had in the meantime gone to the market and bought a new one. Anand felt so sorry about his mother and so much ashamed of himself. After three days, the medicine tube was found in the laundry basket.

Anand's parents decided to go for a vacation and take Anand and his sister along. The train tickets were booked. But on the day of departure, there was a serious commotion in the house right from morning. The tickets were not to be seen anywhere. Instead of feeling excited and happy about the forthcoming vacation, everyone was feeling worried, nervous, and unhappy. The train was to depart in the evening. After a lot of effort and unhappiness, at last, the tickets were found duly wrapped in one of the old newspapers in a corner. Thank God the newspaper had not been thrown away.

It was a wonderful occasion for the family. Anand's elder sister had got engaged and it was a party to announce that. Anand had got stitched a new suit and bought a matching shirt especially for that occasion. On the big day, when Anand started dressing up, he found that the highest button – the tie button – of the shirt was broken. But it was no big deal. Sewing another button on the shirt could take hardly three minutes. Then it was time for those three minutes to start . It got delayed and delayed. The reason was that the sewing needle was not to be seen anywhere. As the time for the party approached, Anand started feeling bad. Eventually he had to wear another shirt; the shirt specially bought for the occasion remained unused on that day. The sewing needle was found but only on the following day.

Then one day Anand met with a funny situation. He had his own room at home. Attached to the room was his restroom. One day it so happened that after he had defecated and it was time to wipe, he found that there was no toilet paper either on the roll (which had been fully used up) or anywhere else in the restroom. He did what he could. But certainly he felt very greatly embarrassed.

One day, Anand was talking to his grandfather. He mentioned some of the embarrassments and setbacks he had to face sometimes. He also mentioned his apprehensions about his becoming a successful physician if these continued.

Looking at Anand's apprehension and frustration, Anand's grandfather said "Always remember that there can be no life without discipline. Discipline always starts with financial discipline. Never spend more than you have except in an emergency. Even when you have to take a debt, repay it as fast as you can."

His grandfather added "Then discipline has other aspects. There should be a place for everything and everything should be at its place. A thing misplaced is a thing lost. Even in madness, there has to be a method. Being methodical avoids setbacks, embarrassments, unnecessary expenditure and waste of time."

His grandfather concluded "Arrange your things considering Value, Volume, Usage, and Criticality and take care of them from time to time. Give maximum attention to high value-low volume things, minimum attention to low value-high volume things, and average attention to the rest. Keep revising your plans as the situation changes. That is the secret to staying cool and achieving success."

One would do well to remember what Anand's grandfather had told him.

Grandpa's Stories about India

THE PRAYING CORNER

NOTE : True

Rai Bahadur Uma Shankar was a man of great wisdom, vision, and dynamism . When India became Independent on August 15, 1947 and the erstwhile princely states were merged into the Indian Union, Rai Bahadur Uma Shankar took voluntary retirement from his work as District Magistrate of the erstwhile State of Bastar and returned to his ancestral home in Bareilly.

Though Rai Bahadur Uma Shankar was a highly learned man, his son Kailash never showed any interest in formal education i.e. beyond the early years. But Rai Bahadur Uma Shankar never felt worried ; he knew that high formal education was not the only attribute for success in life ; with his astute observation he had seen in his son Kailash the great qualities of hard work, enterprise, perseverance, and sociability.

When Rai Bahadur Uma Shankar returned to Bareilly, Kailash was about 33 years old. The then Government of the State of United Provinces (in which Bareilly was located) had just announced big incentives to motivate people to undertake farming in the Terai area (the foothills of Himalayas). When Kailash showed his interest, Rai Bahadur Uma Shankar bought for him about 400 acres of land in Kichha a very small town in Terai 44 miles from Bareilly .

Mr. Kailash started his farming in Kichha. Being a very sociable person with a magnetic personality, soon he developed friendship with almost everyone he met. One of them was the mother of his neighboring farmer whom he always called Jiji (elder sister). The most important thing, which Jiji taught him, was chewing of tobacco.

Mr. Kailash's wife Mrs. Shanti was a wise lady. She knew that tobacco chewing was a very bad habit; besides making the whole place dirty due to frequent spitting , it also led to oral cancer. So she used to make every possible effort to prevent Mr. Kailash from chewing tobacco. Her efforts ranged from most loving and humble requests to mild - hidden threats, to clear strong threats, to mild fights, and eventually to real good fights. But Mr. Kailash had an enviable and admirable love for his wife. He also had remarkable fortitude; he was never upset by anything – at least, not in the matter of tobacco chewing. Mrs. Shanti used to make all her efforts in all sincerity. Mr. Kailash used to listen and watch carefully. Then in all sincerity and seriousness, he resumed tobacco chewing – as if nothing had happened.

But then, time teaches us so much and so many things change with time. Mr. Kailash and Mrs. Shanti gradually had three daughters – Maya, Mona, and Neelu - and a son Anoop. The incident on which this story is based occurred in the summer vacation (May and June) of 1971. By then Maya and Mona had been married. Mona had a son Bobby (about four years and eight months old) and a daughter Baby (about sixteen months old). Maya had a daughter Vini (about three and a half years old). What Mrs. Shanti could not achieve by her requests and rages, smiles and scolding, time started delivering on its own. Mr. Kailash started realizing that by chewing tobacco, he was not only exposing himself to great hazard, but he was also creating a precedence which his children and (now) grand-children could follow. Perhaps he started feeling guilty and worried. Or at least so did it seem. How could Mrs. Shanti and (now the grown up) children feel happier? But there is a joke about habit. It is said that HABIT never goes. You take out H and "A Bit" is there. Remove A and "Bit" is still there. Do away with B and "IT" is there. It is only when "I" goes away (one dies) that habit is gone; so in reality, it never goes.

With the commencement of the summer vacation in 1971, Mr. Kailash and Mrs. Shanti had called the daughters and their families to spend some time with them at Bareilly (Home) and at Kichha (Farm House). The daughters and their families came to Bareilly. They spent a few days at Bareilly. Then all proceeded to the farmhouse at Kichha.

The farmhouse at Kichha was almost a palace located on the side of the State Highway with about 400 acres of farmland adjacent to it. For little kids, it was fun round the clock. Love of grandparents for grandchildren is always natural and abundant. But in view of the fact that Bobby was the eldest grandchild, he was loved too much by all especially by the grandparents. Out of his enormous love, Mr. Kailash used to keep Bobby along almost all the time the child was awake.

Everybody was happy with this arrangement. Mrs. Shanti was happy because she could get sometime to do her household work undisturbed by the grandchildren. Mona was happy to have at least some relief though Baby was still with her. Anoop was happy to get sometime to study. Neelu was a little unhappy to see that her place had been taken away by Bobby; but she used to cool down a little when Bobby called her Mousi (Auntie).

Mrs. Shanti was a very religious lady. She was extremely happy to see that her wonderful husband was also a very religious person. There was a praying place in the house. The praying place had been set up in an armoire in a corner in the study room of Mr. Kailash where he also met informal visitors. It was called the praying corner. Anyone who wanted to pray, used to go to that corner, offer his or her prayers and come back. . As is the tradition in India, everybody used to take a bath, offer his or her prayers, and then take the lunch. Mr. Kailash also followed this. Usually Mr. Kailash liked a siesta after the lunch.

However, Mrs. Shanti always felt a little bewildered by the prayers, which Mr. Kailash apparently used to have after lunch and before his siesta. It was no time for prayers. No one ever prayed like this. Was this some novel idea ? Well, whatever it was, after all, it was only prayer and hence how could anyone even think of any objection in the matter.

One day everybody was sitting and gossiping in the backyard of the farmhouse. Everybody was in a happy mood. Somehow the little talk drifted to prayers. Mrs. Shanti was happy that everybody in the family was religious minded and offered his and her prayers. She went on to add that Mr. Kailash had become so much prayer minded that he offered prayers even after lunch before his siesta. As if this was enough for little Bobby.

The moment Mrs. Shanti said this, little Bobby said with stars twinkling in his eyes "No Nani (Nani is mother's mother). Nana (Nana is mother's father) does not offer his prayers. He secretly chews tobacco". Everybody was amazed. Mrs. Shanti could not believe this. Mr. Kailash felt much embarrassed but his smiling denial confirmed that what Bobby had said was true. However Mrs. Shanti asked little Bobby how he knew. Bobby said that he watched it everyday while lying in his Nana's bed where Bobby slept during the daytime. Mrs. Shanti still could not believe it fully though she had started smelling a rat .She asked Bobby if he could show her where the tobacco was kept. What could make little Bobby - the Junior Sherlock Holmes - happier.

Bobby jumped out of Mrs. Shanti's lap where he was sitting. Holding her hand, he took her to the study room. There he started taking out the heavy books of his Nana. Mrs. Shanti told him not to do that because the books being heavy could not only hurt the little child but also they could also get damaged when (mis) handled by a little child. But little Bobby asked her to wait. He took out a book and said "Nani, tobacco is inside". Mrs. Shanti was so surprised. But her surprise heightened immensely when inadvertently she turned the book and tobacco powder started coming out from somewhere. Bobby looked at his Nani triumphantly with a smile.

Mrs. Shanti was so surprised and shocked. Mr. Kailash was so embarrassed. Everybody present laughed and laughed. Mrs. Shanti scolded Mr. Kailash a lot, of course, with great concern and love. Mr. Kailash only kept smiling.

The lesson of this story is simple. If we want our children and grandchildren not to learn our bad habits, then the remedy is not to hide things from kids. Kids are very smart. They come to know it much sooner than we think. The only proper thing to do is to change ourselves and give up the bad habits at the earliest possible opportunity.

May I tell you that the sweetie pie Bobby is my dearest son Sumeet from whose home computer desk I am recording this event.

Grandpa's Stories about India

LIFE AND CHALLENGE

A young couple known to us was going to have a baby. So my wife Mona and I had gone to the local hospital to cheer them up and see if we could be of any help to them in that hour of need. Everything had already been arranged so well. Hence, there was not much that we could do. The child – a baby boy – was born. We heard his cries. Minutes later, the nurse brought the new born outside to show to us. He was still crying. I asked Mona why was the child crying. Mona said "Whenever a child is born, he cries for sometime and then he is quiet". I asked her "But why is it so". Mona explained "So far the child was there in the womb of his mother for about nine months. There he was completely insulated and protected against everything – heat, cold, air, light, sound, touch, smell, and everything else that there is in the world. Now he has come out of the womb. Hence he is now exposed to and interacting with all those things. He is experiencing things, which he had never experienced in the past. Mainly being new to the experience, he is scared. And that is why he is crying. Don't worry; he will be fine soon". We stayed for sometime. The new mom and the newborn came out. The baby was now quiet . It was about two in the afternoon. We returned home.

****

We went to the hospital again in the evening This time, to deliver a few things needed there. The baby was crying again. I asked Mona what was the matter. She told me that the child was hungry but he was not able to take the mother's milk. I just did not know what to say. I felt sorry, though. The baby continued crying. After a few minutes I asked Mona again if somehow the newborn could be helped. She told me "So far the baby was in the womb of his mother. There, due to the nature's mechanism, he was getting all his requirements effortlessly from his mother; he was not eating or drinking anything directly. Now that he has come out, to survive and grow, he has to drink his mother's milk, which is ideal for him at this stage. But to be able to take his mother's milk, first, he has to learn suckling. That requires some effort to be made by him. So far he has not known making any effort from his side. So he is not liking making of any effort from his side. Since he is hungry, he is crying to tell everyone that he needs to be fed". I asked her what could be done. She replied that nothing was to be or could be done by anyone else. Nature shall teach him how to suckle and he will be fine. We came back. We went there again after two days. The baby was fine. He was suckling and enjoying his mother's milk.

****

He was about thirteen months old. It was such a pleasure to watch him crawl. Sometimes, he stood up holding something near him – chair, table, sofa, bed, and so on - with his two little hands and walked a few steps. On some other occasions, he walked a few steps – two, three, four or sometimes as many as seven – on his own without any other support though toddling all the time. But mostly after walking a few steps, he used to go down on the floor and started crawling on his knees again. His parents, young and inexperienced as they were, used to feel bad when the baby gave up toddling and, under the fear of falling down, resumed crawling. It was at this stage that we went out to our vacation home in Flagstaff for a vacation. We returned after about six weeks. Oh, what a beautiful sight it was. The baby had started walking on his own. Of course when he felt tired, he stopped or sat down. But crawling was almost over. He had learnt walking and discovered the fun of so doing.

****

Another few months passed. The baby grew older and bigger. Until now the baby loved to be held in arms. By the time he was about twenty months old, he started showing his dislike for being held in arms. On the contrary he loved to be left alone – free – so that he could go wherever he wanted to.

****

He had just celebrated his second happy birthday. So far he used to show his dislike and fear whenever he saw some stranger approaching to talk to him or shake hands with him . But whenever he went to the Kid's Corner in the Mall, he used to love that. He loved playing there, he loved playing with other kids, and even
talking (?) to the other kids. He started making friends. Today when he is about 26 months old, he feels so happy to know that he shall be

taken to the Kid's Corner in the Mall where he shall meet so many of his friends.

****

Priya was a little older than three years. Thus far, she had been staying at home and playing with and in the midst of her family members who all loved her so much. But now it was time for her to go to the School. Her parents got her admitted in the finest School in the town. But there was a problem. She did not want to go to the School; . She loved home and family so much and she was so much scared of the unknown School. Every day when it was time for her to go to the School, she started crying. In a crying condition, somehow, she was allured to the School. The moment she returned home, first of all, she told everyone that she cried even in the School. But then gradually crying faded and eventually disappeared totally. A Dental Surgeon today, Priya is awaiting her marriage.

****

He had just passed Grade VIII from a local middle school. He was most happy to know that for High School he was going to a school of national eminence in the hills. Though he never said it, it was clear that he was also feeling sad about going away from his family – his parents and his sister. Encouraged greatly by all, he went to the Boarding School. In the beginning, sometimes, he felt so nostalgic. But gradually he started making friends and liking the School and everything the School offered. He stayed there for four years. He not only felt so happy about his stay and learning but also bloomed into a disciplined boy with a multi-faceted personality possessed of multiple brilliance.

****

After graduating from High School, he successfully competed at a national examination and thus got admitted to an engineering college of eminence. At first he was shocked by the behavior of the other (mainly senior) students during what is called as the "Ragging" period. At times he even felt like quitting. But he knew that it was all a big , though vulgar, joke and , in any case , purely temporary. He maintained his cool and learnt important lessons and skills for the rest of his life besides graduating with Honors.

Ram M. Saxena

****

He had already obtained a Bachelor's degree in Engineering from a prestigious College in India. Encouraged by his parents and inspired by his own wish to do something big in life, he decided to pursue Graduate studies in the USA. Taking the TOEFL was rather easy. But GRE was tough. It was also essential to get a good GRE Score to get the desired Graduate School, Full-funding, and Full Tuition Waiver. The task appeared nearly impossible but he accomplished it with his hard-sustained work notwithstanding the full time heavily demanding job he was holding in India. Today he is an American citizen, holds a prestigious job, and (along with that job) he is almost halfway through with another full-time Graduate degree.

****

But what does all this lead us to ? The message is clear. Life consists of challenges at every stage . When the challenge comes, one feels a little upset because of inertia - he had, hopefully, already settled comfortably in his earlier (present) stage. He also feels apprehensive whether the new transition shall be a happy one or whether he shall be able to successfully face the new challenge and emerge a winner out of it. But by putting in honest , hard and sustained work in a disciplined and patient manner – along with blessings of God – one can successfully face any challenge at any stage of life and emerge a happy winner out of it.

Grandpa's Stories about India

ENCOUNTER WITH A HOLY SPIRIT

It was summer vacation (May and June) of 1955. Summer is always hot in Lucknow but that year it was hotter than ever. In a way, it was good for us; the world famous Dushehri mangoes had ripened earlier and that too so fast that the price came down to Two Annas (0.25 cent as per today's rates) per Seer (930 grams) or a little more than eight pounds for a cent. But in another way, it was also bad. From sunrise to sunset it was so hot that we were not allowed to go out in the open and play. It was such a problem. The worst however used to be the daytime after lunch up to the tiffin (snack) time i.e. between 1 to 4 p.m.

Though we had not decided so formally, it had become almost a daily practice for us to assemble after lunch in the room of Prem, my elder brother. There, myself, my two elder sisters, and two elder brothers chatted and argued about this and that while parents took siesta in their respective bedrooms. However, we had one serious problem. The adjacent room belonged to our eighty year old Baba (grand-father) and it used to be his siesta time also. Hence, we could not talk in our normal loud and clear voices. It was not so much fun to discuss important matters (important at that time) in a low husky voice. But no one could dare to speak loud lest Baba would wake up. Everybody was so scared of Baba. No one had the courage even to stand in front of him; I had never seen anybody even talking to Baba.

One day we were all lamenting over this serious constraint. No one could find a way out. But youngest in the group, I suggested a remedy. I suggested that Baba should also be made an honorable member of the group. Everybody laughed at my innocence. To ridicule me my eldest brother asked me if I could do that. I said I shall try. Everybody laughed again knowing I was being stupid.

But at least at that stage, I was not stupid . I had my own very especial relations with Baba, which I had developed gradually, and secretly unknown to anybody. That needs a little explaining. As said earlier, no one in the family had the courage to face Baba, what to say of talking. All were so scared of him. I could never understand or like this situation. I started watching Baba from behind the door. But then I was soon caught. When he saw me doing this, he smiled. That encouraged me. I also smiled. He called me near him. Extremely scared, I went to him. He patted me on my back and asked me what did I want. I just smiled, shook my head to say No, and came out of his room. Beginning thus, gradually I had made good friends with Baba, which we both liked so much.

Next day I met Baba late in the morning after his prayers. I asked him if he knew any wonderful stories. Beaming with joy he said that he not only knew some wonderful stories but more than that he had some rarest experiences of his own which were more amazing and unbelievable than the stories in the Arabian Nights. I was so happy. I told him that I shall personally come to escort him to the group after lunch.

That day when the group met, I informed everybody that Baba was not only its new honorable member but that he was going to tell us wonderful experiences of his own. At first no one believed. But all were so amazed when within two minutes I brought Baba from the adjacent room. I told Baba that we were all ready to listen to his wonderful personal experiences.

Baba said "This happened many many years ago. Then I was not so old. What to talk of being old. I was a young boy. I must have been about fifteen years at that time (which means it was the year 1890). I had many friends who mostly lived nearby. But there were three of them with whom I was very close. So together we were a good foursome. Those who knew us affectionately and humorously called us the group of four. We studied together, played together, flew kites together, swam together, and did so many things together. I do not even remember after all these years the various activities we did together. In any case, you all shall not be interested in knowing that. You are interested only in your story, I know. So Why should I unnecessarily waste your time. I shall give you the story straight as it all happened.

So we were a group of four good friends. We were all from good families. You know, you cannot be very friendly with those who are much above or much below you in the society. We lived near each other's house. That also made it easier for us to meet each other anytime we wanted to meet. But of course we did not go to anybody at an odd hour; you know, it is impolite to do so.

So one day our group of four friends was sitting together. We were just talking this and that. Somehow the discussion turned to the super-natural elements, ghosts, vampires, witches, and the like. Nowadays if somebody talks about them, people start arguing and saying that they do not exist. But believe me, they exist. Yes, they exist as you will know when I tell you the complete story. So some people nowadays argue that they do not exist. But we know so little even about ourselves. How can we know about everything in the world. Do you want to know the truth ? Well. Do one thing. Go inside a room. Make it completely empty in the middle. Make it completely dark. Lit a lamp in the middle of the room. You will see a big circle duly illuminated by light. Inside this circle you can see everything that there is. This is the area of knowledge of the human race. But beyond the circle of light, it is all-dark. You cannot see if anything exists or does not exist in the dark area. Since you cannot see anything in the dark area, does it mean that nothing exists in the area which is still dark ? Make the light more powerful. The circle of light expands. But yet there is darkness beyond the circle of light. This explains the truth. Truth is what we know. But it does not mean that there is nothing beyond what we know" .Noticing that my eldest brother had started yawning, Baba resumed his story.

"So we were discussing the super-natural elements. One friend said that they did not exist. Another agreed with him. The third friend was not so sure either way. Then they asked me for my opinion. You know if you are discussing something you must take the opinion of all those who are present.. When they asked me, I told them straightaway that they existed and I believed in them. Then the one who had said that they did not exist started laughing. This hurt me because, note it carefully and seriously, it is not a laughing matter; it can even lead to disasters. The discussion turned into an argument. I said that if someone had the courage and was prepared , then we could find out for ourselves. The others took this as a challenge. They were also brave boys and no one was a coward.

They asked me how could we find out. I said that we all could go to the Mosque of the Holy Spirits (Masjid – É – Jinnat). Have you ever heard of that ? No ? It is so surprising and almost a shame that you have not even heard of that Mosque. It is so near this house of ours. You know that we all live in Nawazganj. You also know that nearby is Thakurganj. You go there every day. Go to the main crossing of Thakurganj. Then on the Hardoi Road, go for three miles. Then turn right and enter the dense forest. Be careful. It is a forest with all sorts of things. Go about two miles deep in the forest. There you have the most exquisite white mosque. That is the Mosque of the Holy Spirits.

Normally no one goes to that Mosque. And it is a right thing to do also. No one should go there unnecessarily. And why there only. One should not go anywhere unnecessarily. You should be concerned with your work. However, some very enterprising people have shown the courage of going there. On return they have told us so many things about the Mosque. It is a beautiful Mosque. During the daytime, mostly it is all quiet there. But the things change in the evening.

As soon as the sun sets and the cool breeze starts blowing more so due to the Gomti river near it, things start happening in the Mosque. It is said that so many Jinns (Holy Spirits) come there. They have entertainment – food, song, dance, etc all the night till the daybreak. What ? You don't know who the Jinns are? Well, I shall tell you briefly. One day we all die irrespective of whether we are kings or vagabonds. When we die, then depending upon our deeds we sometimes become blood sucking Vampires (Pishach) or Bad Ghosts (Bhoot) or Holy Spirits

(Jinns). So Jinns are the Holy Spirits. They never say anything to anybody. They never harm anybody. But sure they can harm someone if he disturbs them unnecessarily or teases them. Why should we tease anybody for no reason. Since Jinns are good spirits, they also bestow huge favors on those who show respect to them. The best is to stay away. But if you want some favor, then go to the Mosque late in the afternoon, make an offering of excellent food, lit a lamp, lit the incense sticks, place the fragrant flowers like Jasmine, Rose, Bela, Mogra, etc., and return immediately. You will have good luck some day". At this point, my elder sister asked Baba as to what happened to the story. So Baba returned to the story.

We decided to go to the Mosque next day. We knew that if we tell the people in the family then we shall not only be told not to go but may be we are not allowed even to come out of the houses for a couple of days. So we four decided to go secretly. We wanted to see the Jinns. So we decided to go to the Mosque at a time when they were there.

Next day around noon we left our houses . You know at that time, I used to live in my father's house in the locality called as Astabal (the Stable of the former ruler of the State of Avadh Nawab Asaf –

Ud – Daula) in the Yahyaganj area. We walked about two miles and reached Gol Darwaza in Chowk. We took some cold syrup. We started walking again. About three miles more and we came to the main crossing of Thakurganj. There we had some cold water. Now onwards was lonely. We kept walking for three miles more leaving behind us the famous Kalyanji Temple. We reached the place where the forest began. We turned right and continued to walk. No body was feeling any fatigue; the excitement was so much. Moreover, all the time, we were talking about the super-natural elements and the Jinns in particular who bestowed enormous favors on those who served them sincerely.

At last we saw the beautiful white minarets of the Mosque so majestically rising into the blue sky. As we neared, we saw some part of the Mosque. Though none of us told the other, each had started feeling a little scared. But we were not much scared because we were not going to do anything bad to anybody. We kept marching forward. Then we almost reached the gate of the Mosque . The gate had such a beautiful carving all over that we felt totally enchanted by that . We had hardly started discussing with each other as to what to do next when suddenly something happened.

There was the gate of the Mosque. It had a staircase consisting of about thirty steps. On the top of the staircase, there was a very tall man. He was an old man. He had snow-white long hairs. He had a snow white long beard and similar moustache. He wore an ankle long white robe. In an angry but very heavy voice, he asked us why did we come.

For a moment we thought that he was some priest of the Mosque. But I recognized him at once. He had a nasal voice. That was a certain characteristic of the Jinns; they always have a nasal voice. I told my friends to run away. And we started running as fast as possible. We were all very young. So we all ran very fast . We kept running and running till we came to Thakurganj. We took a short break. But we were scared that the Jinn could be chasing us. So we started running again. It was only when we came to Gol Darwaza in Chowk that we could feel out of danger. As you know very well, Chowk is the main market and normally in busy crowded places, Jinns don't come for anything. We ate some sweets in Chowk . Then we returned to our homes.

When we returned to our homes, the Sun had already set and it had started to turn dark. However, we found some alibi and kept quiet. Even in the night when I was sleeping, I dreamt of the Jinns chasing me. But dreams are dreams. When scared by them I woke up in the middle of the night, my mother could understand that I had some bad dream. She told me to drink some cold water. I did that. I also knew one more trick to protect myself. Silently in my mind I recited Hanuman Chaleesa. You know, nothing in the whole world can harm you if you recite Hanuman Chaleesa which clearly says – GHOSTS AND VAMPIRES DO NOT COME NEAR WHEN THE NAME OF HANUMAN IS RECITED".

Baba had completed his story. He went back to his room. We all dispersed. But in the middle of the night, I not only had to get up and drink cold water but quietly in my mind I also recited Hanuman Chaleesa because I felt chased by the Jinns.

Though I have narrated the story as far as possible in the words of Baba, I am seriously constrained by the fact that I am merely writing this story on the computer whereas Baba had told it to us in person with all the excitement and actions which I cannot present here. However, I am telling myself to feel contented by one thing. I am sure that when I will die, meet Baba in person and tell him that I have told his story to my grandsons, he will give me the same affectionate smile which long ago I had seen on his face from behind a door.

The lesson of the story is clear. The area of human knowledge is very limited; the area of our ignorance is much wider. The more we learn the more we discover how little we know. We should not unnecessarily argue about something, which we do not know. There is so much more which man has yet to know.

Grandpa's Stories about India

LALA

NOTE : True

In simple words, Chowk means the most important crossroad obviously located in the heart of the town. Chowk in Lucknow was the heart of the town during the regime of the Nawabs of Avadh. Even today, Chowk is a very important market of Lucknow; Jewelry Shops (called as Sarrafa), Wholesale Chickan Garment Shops, and Moneylenders are still located in the Chowk market. Chowk has also been the most favorite place for the lovers of sweets . For decades together (until the 1960s) there were only two shops, which were patronized most by the lovers of sweets. Both were located in the Chowk area. One of these was the shop of Lala Tika Ram inside Gol Darwaza (the Round Gate) and the other was that of Lala Ram Asrey.

Lala Ram Asrey's (residence cum) shop was located in the Ban – Wali – Gali in Chowk. When we move on the Hardoi Road from Gol Darwaza then after about 200 yards on the left hand side, there is a narrow lane in which only pedestrians are allowed . This is Ban – Wali – Gali. Go about 200 yards in it and on the left hand side we have the (residence cum) shop of Lala Ram Asrey. The lane is so narrow and the building is so high, that one cannot see the top of the building without the fear of his cap (called as Topi) falling which is not something which is liked anywhere in the World including of course Lucknow.

I don't exactly remember how old Lala Ram Asrey's shop is. But according to my guesstimate, the founder Lala Ram Asrey around the year 1900 must have established it. He brought enormous fame to his sweets. But he died early. His equally graceful, unassuming and kind son Lala Tulsi Ram took over. He continued to expand and diversify the business. For many years, I used to know him. But he too died early. He had two sons; the elder was Lala Anand Bihari and the younger was Lala Suman . This story is about Lala Anand Bihari.

For the first time, I met Lala Anand Bihari Gupta (we always and affectionately called him Lala; the word Lala means the rich merchant) in the year 1955 when I joined Class XI as a student of Commerce in the Kali Charan Inter College, Lucknow. We were in the same class. We were both important. I was important because I had gone to that College from Jubilee Inter College, which was a very prestigious College, and no one was prepared to believe that a student from Jubilee could join Kali Charan. Lala was important because he was not only son of a very rich merchant but also because he was the fattest boy in the College. Soon I discovered that Lala was a very graceful, a most unassuming, and a very kind person just like his father and grandfather.

When I saw Lala for the first time, I smiled in my mind. But perhaps the smile was too strong. Hence a part of it also appeared on my face. I tried to cover it with the impression of "Pleased" to meet you but Lala was perhaps too familiar with it; he must have been seeing it on the face of everyone he met for the first time. He did not mind it. More so because I was the youngest boy in the Class.

Gradually we came closer. Lala was a bright student and participated actively and brilliantly in the discussions. I was also good at my studies.

Whenever there was a celebration in the family, my parents used to ask me to buy sweets from the market and the "market" always meant "only" the shop of Lala Ram Asrey. Even by exception, sweets from any other shop were not acceptable. Whenever this happened, I met Lala at the shop. He was always there helping his father Lala Tulsi Ram who was alive at that time.

Sometimes in the evening I went for a walk to Kuria Ghat (one of the banks) of Gomti river. The shortest and most convenient route from my residence in Nawazganj to Kuria Ghat was via Ban – Wali – Gali , Gol Darwaza and Victoria Park (earlier known as the Company Park i.e. the parade ground of the army of the East India Company). While going to and fro, I mostly met Lala.

These meetings outside the classroom brought us closer. We became good friends. In 1957 we both graduated from Intermediate (Class XII) and we both decided to join the two year B Com Program in the internationally renowned local University of Lucknow. We chose the same electives and were in the same batch. I was working round-the-clock for first rank. Lala also took his studies seriously. This brought us still closer.

Then in 1959 we both graduated from B Com. I joined the two-year M Com Program . But Lala dropped further studies. He came from a very rich family with a very well established business of their own. Hence there was no need for him to acquire further education. In fact his absence from the shop (when he was in the University for his B Com classes) caused a setback to his aging and ailing father.

Though Lala gave up further studies my meetings with him continued to be very frequent. Our friendship became thicker and better everyday. What a wonderful person he was. There was a smile of welcome on his face whenever I saw him. It was not possible for me to pass through the Ban – Wali – Gali without stopping at his shop, meeting Lala, talking to him for a couple of minutes, and enjoying the free treat of finest sweets of my life – the inimitable Doodhia, the matchless Malai Ki Gilaori, the exceptionally tasteful Tirangi Barfi, the baffling Santrey Ki Barfi, and my favorite Halwa Sohan besides Dalmoth to salten the mouth and drink water before taking two pairs of the famous Maghai Pan. Even though it has been almost four decades since then, the memory is live in my mind and the taste is fresh in my mouth.

But once in the midst of this wonderful and sweet friendship something happened. Perhaps it was somewhere in the vicinity of 1960. As usual, I was returning from my evening walk from Kuria Ghat. I halted at Lala's shop to say hello. Even in the midst of his preoccupation with work, we chatted about this and that. But suddenly I found that he was angry. Not only that, he told me clearly that in spite of his most courteous behavior, I was using a very rude language. I was shocked because I could not even dream of talking to someone – and that too someone like
him – in a rude language.

I asked Lala what wrong had happened. He told me that he was always addressing me as AAP (Respectful You) but I was addressing him as ABE (a Very Rude way of addressing someone). I immediately understood the matter. Actually there was a big misunderstanding.

In Lucknow when two extremely dear friends talk to each other, it is quite common for them to address each other as "AMAN YAAR" which means "Oh, you dear friend". These words are typical of Lucknow and due to their usage, a person from Lucknow can be easily recognized anywhere. It is also not uncommon for these wonderful words to be twisted a little for FURTHER SWEETNESS; the address then being "AMEN YAAR". What happened is that I was saying "AMEN YAAR" and my wonderful sweet friend Lala heard "ABE YAAR".

I was shocked beyond words. I was too pained to see that my wonderful friend Lala could imagine and believe that I could use the rude words. Totally stunned, I kept quiet. After a little talk, I returned. Because of my shock, I could never even think of clearing up the matter. However whenever we met after that, we met as the same old dear friends.

Soon I moved out of Lucknow . Whenever I visited Lucknow, I always met Lala, the same wonderful dear friend. Some years ago, he too died handing over the big business to his son.

But the above incident had a deep impact on my mind. I stopped using the typically Lucknow words "AMAN YAAR" or "AMEN YAAR" or anything like that and confined to "AAP" which is very respectful.

The story tells us that we should be very careful about our words .Often people speak in such a tone that I cannot make out whether it is CAN or CAN'T; why not simply say CAN and CANNOT.

Grandpa's Stories about India

THEFT

NOTE : True

    Once somebody had asked me "What is maturity" and then proceeded to add that it is the mental attitude one develops after undergoing five experiences viz. Constructing own house, Contesting an election, Marrying a daughter, Getting hurt in an accident, and Becoming victim of a theft.
    I had closely witnessed my late father constructing his house; I decided not to construct one of my own. Long ago I had read somewhere that according to Dr. Samuel Johnson religion was the last resort of the scoundrel in the nineteenth century and now it is politics. I would better not comment on what Dr. Johnson said. However, I always felt that politics was for some special people. In spite of lots of inspirations, assurances, and even threats I have not been able to accept the idea that I am anything above the ordinary man. Hence I never entered politics and never contested any election. I married my only daughter in 1994. The experience of accident is discussed in the succeeding story. This story, therefore, deals with my experience of theft.
    But before proceeding to do that, a word about maturity. I have come to think that one can be said to have attained maturity when he acquires courage to change the things he can, serenity to accept the things he cannot change, and wisdom to know the difference between the two. The truth is that one never reaches that stage but ideals are meant for inspiring people to strive in that direction. Now the theft experience.
    It was perhaps August of 1977. At that time I was a Lecturer in the University of Jodhpur. I had received a call for interview for the post of Reader in the Himachal Pradesh University in Shimla. Leaving my wife and two little children at Jodhpur, I went to Shimla to attend the Interview knowing it well that within a couple of days I shall return to Jodhpur.
    At Shimla I stayed in my favorite Meghdoot Hotel. The next day when I went to attend the Interview, the local Professor and Chairman of the Department told me that on my return journey I was to go via

Meerut (near Delhi) where my wife had already gone to visit my seriously ill mother – in – law. I attended the Interview and left immediately for Delhi and Meerut.

At Meerut I stayed for two days. There I met my wife Mona. She told me that she had received a telegram from her parents informing her that her mother was seriously ill. Hence she had left the two little children at the house of a senior friend and she had come to Meerut. When I asked her how she came, she told me that at such a short notice no reservation was available on the railways. Hence she had to travel unreserved by bus from Jodhpur to Jaipur (200 miles) and again by bus from Jaipur to Delhi (200 miles) and yet again by bus from Delhi to Meerut (50 miles). I was shocked and pained but it was all over. My mother – in – law was really serious but with the best efforts of the best available physicians, she soon improved substantially. My wife Mona and I left Meerut and came to Delhi.

We were traveling under very strange circumstances. We did not have any reservation on 93 UP, the train from Delhi to Jodhpur; it was scheduled to depart from Delhi at about 8 p.m. and arrive at Jodhpur next day around noon covering a distance of about 400 miles in about 16 hours.

Since we did not have any reservation, we knew that it was going to be very tough for us to get some accommodation in the train. We needed some accommodation and that too enough for at least one person to lye down. So we came to Delhi Junction a little early.

Gradually the crowd on the platform increased. By the time the train was expected to come on the platform, the crowd had become heavy. For the sake of convenience, I had engaged two porters though we had only one iron trunk and one bedding with us. One of the porters suggested the strategy. He suggested that my wife and one porter would wait on the platform with luggage. The second porter and myself shall go a few yards beyond the platform beside the railway track on which the train was supposed to come to the platform. The porter told me that by the time the train reaches the platform, it becomes very slow and it will be so easy to board the moving train and capture a berth for my wife and myself. I agreed.

But we were not the only wise (?) people. There were many more. As we reached the desired place I found that there as well, we had a small crowd. The train came. Certainly it had slowed down. But still it was moving. Then there were so many other people who were jostling with each other to enter the moving train. I tried my best to grab the handle of the unreserved compartment. But my hand slipped. Normally I should have fallen on the ground. But I did not fall. As the train was rather very slow and further as I am a rather tall person, instead of falling on the ground, I stumbled and ran a few steps in a totally unstable manner due to the momentum of the moving train. . I still remember somebody shouting "You will die, O fool". Yes, it was my folly. My glasses had fallen on the ground. Surprisingly, I got them intact.

When I recovered from the immediate shock, I found that the porter with me had already grabbed a berth and he was shouting for me to come and engage it. I quickly did it. But in the meantime so many others had come. All that I could get was space for two persons to sit. The first porter brought my luggage and escorted my wife to my berth in the train. I sat on the edge of the berth and my wife occupied the adjacent seat. We kept the bedding overhead and the iron box under our seats as everybody does. Hardly did we sit in the train that it departed.

A few minutes after the train departed from the platform, a man apparently in his early sixties, came to the place where we were sitting. He was selling bed covers. He spread a large bed cover on our knees for people to see. We were simply not interested in such things. For a moment I felt that someone has removed my iron box beneath my berth . At once I removed the bed cover and saw below the berth. The box was not there. I looked up. The man was not there. When the man spread the bed cover, one of his accomplices removed the box. Before I raised my head again, the man selling the cloth ran away. I went here and there in the compartment. There was no trace of the box or the man. I am convinced the man had moved to another compartment in the moving train and his accomplice had thrown the box outside from the window of the moving train.

I told my wife that someone had stolen our iron box. She was also amazed and shocked. We started recalling what we had in that box. My wife told me that there was some jewelry. There were some coins of foreign countries, which was a part of my son's coin collection. There was some cash. It had many of my books, which I had carried with me to Shimla. There were some sarees, woolens, and other clothes. But in spite of the quarter century which has elapsed since then, perhaps the thing which we still consider to be the most important and valuable contained in that iron box was the three Gold Medals and one Chancellor's Medal which had been awarded to me when I was a student at the University of Lucknow. I still miss it. I wish I had them with me so that I could show them to my two grandsons to inspire them to do better in life.

The next train stoppage was at Rewari. At the Police Outpost, no one was prepared to talk. In the meantime, the train started again. Next day at noon we reached Jodhpur.

At Jodhpur, I lodged a report with the Police. They listened to it patiently. However, out of their sympathy for me, they took from me some tip money for tea, snacks, etc so that they could look into the matter expeditiously. The result of their efforts is still awaited. I was not shocked or surprised. I did not expect anything from the Police.

Then we started thinking about the reason behind the theft. The main reason was as apparent as Sun on a clear day. It was mainly MY fault. No, it was not a fault. It was a BLUNDER. At that time, I was very fond of wearing gold rings. At that time, when the theft took place, I had four gold rings on my fingers. The thieves must have thought that I was some jeweler carrying lots of jewelry and cash. And that tempted them to raid with a whole gang.

For years together, we kept thinking of our mistakes due to which the tragedy took place. Some of the lessons, which we learnt as a result of this theft, may be mentioned here for the benefit of others.

It is never safe to travel in the train without proper reservation. It is better to postpone departure than to travel unreserved. Whatever the situation may be, one should never lose self-composure and cool; rushing in a great haste for anything always enhances the risk of tragedies. It does not make any difference to the World if we are late by a few days even in tragic situations. One should not wear or carry any jewelry under any circumstances when traveling by train; if one wears it, it amounts to inviting the thieves and robbers. One should never try to board a moving train because in a fraction of a moment one can die or become permanently handicapped. Not that one does not know these things; we all know them too well. It is only that due to the excitement of the moment, we tend to lose our guard. And that is exactly the moment when such tragedies occur.

Grandpa's Stories about India

ACCIDENT

NOTE : True

In September 1965, the Indo – Pakistan War took place. At that time I was a Lecturer with the University at Jodhpur. For fourteen nights without break, Jodhpur was bombarded by F – 86 Saber Jets and F – 104 Star Fighters of the PAF (Pakistan Air Force).. We , i.e. my newly married wife Mona and me, spent fourteen nights in the trench in front of our house in the Polo ground locality of Jodhpur. When the PAF planes came, there was a rising and falling sound of the siren, which was a signal that bombardment was going to begin. Hearing that we rushed to the trenches. Then hundreds of tracers were fired illuminating the dark Jodhpur sky with brilliant red lights to locate the PAF bombers; this was followed by the firing of the AAC Guns (Anti Air Craft Guns). The PAF planes dropped the bombs, and went back. Then there was the All Clear signal – a long siren gradually going from high to low pitch.. In short, we acquired a very vivid and first hand experience of bombardment.

This was the reason why we took the decision we did when the Indo – Pakistan war of 1971 took place. We knew too well what it could be and what it could mean for us.

At the time of Indo – Pakistan War of 1971 I was still a Lecturer with the University at Jodhpur. I distinctly remember that it was December 5, 1971. I was running high temperature of about 104 d due to flu. My son Sumeet (a little over five years) , my daughter Seema (a little less than two years) and my wife Mona were with me. We had taken our meals and gone to bed though myself and Mona had not slept yet.

Suddenly there was a very loud thunderous sound of explosion. Even the doors and glass panes of the windows shook noisily. The walls shook with violent vibrations and the various things in the cupboards rattled noisily. We knew that the War could start any day. And we had the experience of bombardment in 1965. So in a moment I told Mona that the War had started and the sound we had heard was that of the PAF bombers dropping bombs on Jodhpur. I immediately wore my nightgown and went on the top of the single level house in the Polo-ground.

I looked in the direction of the IAF Station. There was a huge fire from ground to the sky. I could also see many neighbors on the street and housetops. Every one wanted to know exactly what had happened. We had two guesses. One, IAF Station was bombarded. Two, some PAF plane was shot down. But within moments we got clarity.

After every four – five minutes we started hearing sounds of big explosions. And that continued for hours together. In the meantime, some enthusiasts went to the IAF Station . On return they told us that the PAF planes had hit the Kerosene Dump of the Indian Army. It was the kerosene drums, which were exploding like huge bombs after every four – five minutes.

This created a very serious and totally intolerable problem for all of us including our little son Sumeet. Whenever a drum exploded with a thunderous sound, little Seema cried and cried. Before she could calm down, the next explosion occurred.. This continued for almost the entire night. Sometimes when Seema cried, Sumeet also got up weeping. Mona and I discussed the matter.

We knew that the War was likely to continue for sometime; in any case , it was not going to be over in a day or two. We both had a perfect first hand experience of the 1965 War. We knew that there shall be bombardment every night, which shall always make children wake up in the middle of their sleep and cry . We were not the least worried about ourselves. Since we had faced the terrible bombardment in 1965, we had become hardened (I am too strongly tempted to quote Urdu poet Ghalib who says that so many difficulties fell on me that they became easy – MUSHKILEN MUJH PER PAREEN ITNI KI AASAN HO GAYEEN). But we were worried about the children.

As Mona and I discussed the matter, the night gave way to the morning. While taking our morning tea, we decided to leave Jodhpur at once for Bareilly, if possible , for the duration of the War. I got the berths reserved and by the afternoon train we left for Bareilly.

Though the War ended on December 16, 1971, we stayed at Bareilly up to December 30, 1971.

On December 31, 1971 we were scheduled to leave Bareilly for return to Jodhpur. The arrangement was that we shall go by the U.P.

Grandpa's Stories about India

Government Roadways Bus from Bareilly to Delhi and from there, board the train for Jodhpur. But things were not destined thus.

To catch the bus at 11 a.m., we left home early and reached the Bus Stand by 10.15 a.m. The Bus was to come from Pilibhit and go to Delhi. It came at the proper time. We got the best seats i.e. full berth just behind the Driver (in India, motor vehicles are right hand driven).

Just as the Bus was about to depart, the domestic servant Noni came. We told the Driver to please wait for a moment. We were surprised to see him. He had brought the small kerosene lamp I wanted to take to Jodhpur with me but which I had forgotten. The lamp was taken. But my father-in-law (we always called him Papa) and Mona were angry while I simply smiled. There was a reason for this strange behavior. India is a country with a very rich cultural heritage of thousands of years; the heritage also includes many strange beliefs. It is a widely and well-accepted belief that while leaving for a journey one should not carry kerosene or kerosene lamp/hurricane lantern; if one does, it is a bad omen. Moreover, at the time of departure, one should not see a person with only one eye otherwise, being a bad omen, it is sure to bring bad luck. We got BOTH when Noni came. He not only brought the kerosene lamp but he had only one eye. That is why my Papa and Mona had become angry. Since I have never believed in such things, by and large, I smiled to watch the anger of the two. The Bus left Bareilly.

Every society has its own culture i.e. the way people live and behave. In India, people like to talk to everyone they meet in sufficient detail . And we were no exception. On our left hand side, a very finely dressed gentleman in his sixties was sitting wearing a beautiful suit and a tie, almost like me. He also had expensive suitcases apparently from some foreign country. I could not prevent myself from asking him where he was going (What a question ? – we knew that the Bus was going to Delhi). He was a very fine and pleasant person. He smiled at my innocent enquiry. Then said that he was going to Delhi to catch a plane in the evening for London where he lived. Then we discussed this and that. The Driver became too friendly with him and he also gave some foreign cigarettes to the Driver to smoke. The Bus, now more than fully occupied i.e. about 60 passengers, kept moving on.

When the Bus halted at Moradabad, we took our packed lunch. Around 2 p.m. the Bus left Moradabad on way to Delhi. As I said we were occupying the berth just behind the Driver. On the berth Mona was sitting near the window. Next to her was our dear son Sumeet. And then I was seated with our dear daughter Seema in my lap. The Bus, being a long distance Bus, was going fast.

We had left Moradabad about 9 miles behind and we were passing through the village of Majhola. The Bus was in its full speed. Every passenger was enjoying himself. Mostly people were chatting with each other. Some boys sitting somewhere in the rear were, however, singing. They were perhaps a small part of some marriage party. Mona had given me a Paan (Beetle Leaf), which I had taken, and she was enjoying one herself.

Suddenly I felt a jolt. Since I was sitting in the first row, I could very easily and clearly see that the jolt was on account of the Bus suddenly moving a little to the right hand side. I wondered why. Immediately I saw that a man on his bicycle had entered the road. He was at an angle of 135 degree from our Bus i.e. he was entering the road from northwest. That was totally illegal because in India one goes on the left hand side of the road (By the way, is it not really funny that LEFT is RIGHT and RIGHT is WRONG). He apparently wanted to cross the road before our Bus reached that spot so that he could ride on the left hand side of the road i.e. from the side of Delhi to the side of Moradabad. I was shocked because I knew that it could lead to an accident. However, I had the hope that our Bus shall be able to cross that point much earlier being much faster.

The cyclist came deeper into the road towards our Bus. The Bus moved a little further to the right hand side apparently to avoid and escape the cyclist. I was horrified because I could see people on the right part of the road coming from the opposite side. Now it appeared to me that we were likely to have an accident in which some of us could get hurt. But still I had the hope of escaping the accident

(Besides Forgetfulness, HOPE is the best and the most important characteristic of the Human Being; up to the last breath, human being is hopeful). Quickly I looked around. Everything was as it was.

The cyclist came deeper into the road towards our Bus. The Driver moved the Bus further to the right hand side of the road. Now I knew that we were going to have an accident most probably by colliding with the cyclist. It also occurred to my mind that we could also get hurt in the accident, which was now imminent and totally unavoidable. Hope of escape was almost gone.

Then I saw the trunk of a huge tree almost adjacent to the front windshield of our Bus. My heart missed a beat. I knew the much-apprehended Accident was here and we were likely to die in it. All the false hopes, which I had been harboring thus far suddenly, disappeared; my mind accepted the inevitable. For the first time in my life, I saw Death, the greatest truth of life, on my eyelashes.

And then it happened – the Accident. Our Bus going in full speed collided with extreme force with the trunk of the huge tree outside the road on our right hand side. The Bus came to a halt suddenly as a result of the collision. Describing the events here after more than 30 years has certainly taken some time. But then it all happened within a few seconds. With my mental eyes I can still see the trunk of the huge tree almost adjacent to the front windshield of our Bus while I am still sitting inside the Bus with my family on the front berth just behind the Driver. With the ears of my mind, I can still hear the enormous noise of the Bus colliding with the trunk of the tree. During the last 30 years, I have seen these images and heard these sounds innumerable times.

Hardly a second later, I regained my consciousness. I thanked God I was alive. I looked in my lap. It was empty. I became totally lifeless. Seema, who had been sitting in my lap all along, was not there. The next moment I saw the Driver jumping out of the Bus with Seema in his arms. I returned to life.

I looked to my right. Sumeet was standing just near the seat where he had been sitting; he was very nervous. Next I saw Mona. She was in her seat. But her mouth was bleeding badly . When the Bus stopped all of a sudden, then due to its enormous momentum and impact, Mona's face had collided with great force with the steel wall of the Bus, which had damaged her lower front teeth . First I asked a man to help Sumeet jump out of the Bus. Sumeet went out. Then I asked Mona to jump out of the Bus. I told her to do it at once because I knew that the petrol tank of the Bus could burst any moment and the Bus could catch fire; on that moment I saw Death on my nose tip.

Mona told me that she had been badly hurt in her left leg. I told her to try her best and go out at once. She asked me to accompany her. I tried to stand up. But my bleeding left leg was caught in the steel bars, which had bent due to the accident. I asked some people to help. The bars were removed. I tried to stand up. But I fell on my seat. My left knee had been badly hurt .I saw death hanging by a thin thread very near my eyes as the Bus could catch fire any moment burning many of us and surely me because due to the injured knee, I could not move on my own. Mona told me that I had sustained serious injuries. I kept quiet. Then some people helped Mona and I get out of the Bus. It was at this stage that I looked around inside the bus. The graceful old passenger for London was lying dead in a pool of blood. The Bus was full of blood and injured people. People were crying and shouting. There was total chaos. I could not stand. So I told my helpers to help me sit on the ground outside the road but very near the Bus. They helped. We were out of the Bus.

I sat on the ground bleeding. Mona, bleeding, stood near me with Seema in her arms. Sumeet stood near us. So many people had gathered near us. That was good and bad, both. I was extremely worried about my luggage on the top of the Bus. In that big crowd and utter confusion, any one could steal anything. I knew that in our iron box we had all our jewelry and a good amount of cash.. I requested some people to bring my luggage from the Bus top. They helped. I got my luggage.

Then I looked at my left leg. It had been badly hurt on the knee. I could understand that in all probability it was an open fracture. I thanked God for Sumeet who was totally unhurt and Seema who had got only a bump on her forehead. That gave me some strength. I guessed that Mona too had not sustained any injury, which could endanger her life. That gave me further strength. I requested some people to stop the first available truck going from Delhi side to Moradabad side . With God's grace, we got a truck at once. It was also totally empty.

People near us wanted to put us in the back of the truck first of all. There were two reasons. One , we were very well dressed up. Two, I was the only person who was in full senses and who could talk. There had been an extremely bad tragedy in the Bus. Much later we learnt that six persons had died on the spot and about forty had been badly injured.

I refused to be helped first. I told them to put those people first who had sustained very serious injuries. I told them that comparatively I was much better. Even to this day it gives me a little peace of mind to recall that due to the inspiration from God I did a good deed on that day. They were surprised. But they obeyed; there was no time to be lost. I called the truck driver and asked him to take us to Moradabad. He was greatly worried that he could be detained or troubled by the Police. However, he agreed to drop us at Moradabad District Hospital.

On way to Moradabad District Hospital, I asked the Driver to stop for a few minutes. I sent a man from the street to the office of my brother-in-law Suresh that was located on the side of the road itself. Suresh came at once. I handed over Mona's purse to him, which contained the jewelry and cash. Then I asked the Driver to proceed at once to the District Hospital. We reached the Hospital. We were all taken out of the truck. The truck driver moved away even before I could thank him. May God bless him. If he had not helped on that occasion, may be I would not have been alive today to record the event.

For a few minutes it was all chaos at the Hospital. However, soon things started moving. I told the Doctors first of all to examine Seema and put medicine on the injury on her forehead. I told the Doctors to give first aid to Mona. With Seema in her arms, bleeding Mona was taken to the Dental Department. I was moved to the Orthopedics Department.

They put me on the operation table in the Operation Theatre (OT). Then a young handsome Doctor came and asked me what had happened. I told him briefly what had happened. He told me not to worry as the needful could be done without any problem in no time. I asked him to tell me honestly and frankly the type of injuries I had sustained, the broad treatment I was to get, and the tentative time for which I was likely to be in bed . He hesitated for a moment. Then he told me that I had a compound fracture of my left patella and I was likely to be in bed for about two to three months. I remember very well that I had asked him if my leg was to be amputated. He told me that it was not needed. He told me that he was going to operate then and there.

I told the Orthopedic Physician not to do that. He asked me why and what did I want. I told him to give me first aid and seal my wounds well so that I could reach Bareilly safely . I told him that at Moradabad there was none to take proper care of us for such a long time (my sister-in-law Maya and her husband Suresh both were holding full time jobs) and at Bareilly I had my in-laws who had enormous resources. First the Doctor did not agree. But then he could understand. He agreed to give me a LAMA Discharge (Left Against Medical Advice). I said that was fine.

The Doctor gave me first aid. All the time we were chatting happily. He had done his M. S. (Orthopedics) from Vellore Medical College, which is a premier medical institution of India. That gave me further peace of mind. I told him that I was lucky to have a skilled and wonderful person like him. Much later in 1990 when Mona and I were on a one-month trip to South India, I made it a point to stop at Vellore Medical College and pay my respects to that institution whose alumni had saved my life in 1971.

Though the Doctor gave me first aid, I was not released. The Police had intervened because it was a serious case of accident. The police intervention delayed my departure for Bareilly. I knew I was becoming worse with every delay because septic formation was going on endangering my life. I tried my best but the police did not agree. They wanted to use me as their only witness. I could see that.

Immediately I called the senior most policeman on the spot. I told him that I had neither seen anything nor heard anything and neither I knew anything nor I had anything to say about the accident. I told the Police Officer that my life was in danger due to the delay caused by the police and that he shall be personally liable if anything happened to me. Now he could understand what I was saying. He said that all that he wanted was to help me. I told him that if at all police wanted to help me then the best they could do was to inform my sister's husband Mr. R.K.Saksena, P.C.S. (Judicial) Additional District Judge at Bareilly about what had happened and also that we were reaching Bareilly in the evening. The police officer was surprised to hear this. He asked me why I wanted him to do this. I told him that I could not move and that Police Wireless System could convey the message from Moradabad to Bareilly in a moment and the Bareilly police could make a local call within another one minute while a call by me through the normal public telephone system could take hours and hours. Now he knew whom he was talking to. He agreed. We were allowed to go after I signed my police statement of "Nothing" said earlier.

Suresh and Maya hired a taxi. Suresh told me that under instructions from Papa, we were going to Mission Hospital Bareilly. We left Moradabad at about 9.45 p.m. The Driver was driving very carefully. But the road was damaged after every few yards .On those spots the taxi bumped causing me pain in the damaged knee. We reached Clara Swain Methodist Mission Hospital Bareilly (if I remember correctly it is a Hospital with American support and with state-of-the-art facilities) at about 12.45 on the morning of January 1, 1972, the New Year Day.

At Mission Hospital Bareilly, there were about 150 persons related to my wife Mona. They had heard about the accident and they had come to enquire about our welfare and offer whatever help they could. I was completely overwhelmed and felt so much reassured. I remember my mother-in-law rushing to me in tears only to make a few tears roll out of my eyes as well – for the first time since the accident occurred.

The efficiency at the Mission Hospital Bareilly was amazing. At once they told me that they were separately taking care of Mona and that I was being taken to the Operation Theatre (OT) for an operation. As the stretcher on which I was placed started moving a cousin Mama (brother of mother) of Mona asked me if I wanted to say anything. I still remember the words I had spoken "I will come back. My children are too little. I cannot die. Let's go". It was only much later that I came to know that I survived ONLY because I had refused to die.

I was moved to the table in the OT. There were so many people wearing green masks. They began action at once. Then came the Chief Orthopedic Physician Dr. Shaw. He was to operate on me. He started talking to me. He introduced himself. He asked me who I was, where did I belong to, what did I do, etc. I asked him the same question, which I had asked the Doctor at Moradabad. He gave me the same answer. I very well remember having told Dr. Shaw that I was mentally prepared for amputation of my left leg if it was essential to save my life; I had also told him that I was a teacher, not an actor, and I could very well do with only one leg. The Doctor told me not to worry though even at that moment I could see a thin shadow of worry on his face.

The operation work started. They cleaned the wound on my left knee and did all those surgical things. Then Dr. Shaw told me "There is compound fracture of the left patella . It has been broken T-wise into three pieces. We will repair the patella. We will insert two steel nails crosswise, which shall be taken out after sometime. We will also insert a wire to hold the three pieces of the patella together. That wire may or may not be taken out later. Is that fine ?" I told them it was fine with me. I also asked the Doctor how long I was going to be in bed before I could resume my teaching work. Dr. Shaw smiled and said "For now, just relax".

The surgery team continued to do its work. Dr. Shaw was working and talking to me simultaneously. He told me that he had to leave the New Year Eve Party and come for my operation. I told him that I was sorry to hear that. Then I told him with a smile that once I was normal, I shall invite him for a lavish party of alcoholic drinks (which I loved so much at that time) to compensate Dr. Shaw for the evening. He too smiled and said that he did not take alcoholic drinks. He added that in the party he was the only one who fortunately did not drink and hence it was easy for him to come and operate. That was for the first time in my life when I realized that drinking was not always good; what could become of me if even Dr. Shaw had been drinking. I knew the answer. I could die.

The surgery continued for many hours. Then Dr. Shaw told me that I needed rest and hence I was being put to sleep. I said OK. It was about 4 in the morning on the New Year Day. They gave me an injection. I slept. I don't know what happened afterwards. (After a long time Papa told me that after the surgery was over, he had asked Dr. Shaw about my condition. Dr. Shaw had said "We have done our best. Rest is in the hands of God. So pray". When Papa enquired if there was any infection in my body, he was told that there was a lot of it. Then when Papa asked about the chances of my survival, he was told "Five percent, because there is so much of infection". This happened because of the delay at Moradabad. Again after a very long time Dr. Shaw told me that on the day of the operation, my body temperature and blood pressure were so high that according to the norms of surgery, no operation could be performed. However, since my general condition was excellent and I was chatting gladly, they took a chance, succeeded and I could remain alive).

When I started regaining my consciousness I felt that Death was still hanging with a very weak thread above my head. I felt that I was still on the OT table (or something like that). I saw some daylight but could not make out whether it was morning or evening or a daytime on a cloudy day. My left leg was under plaster from the top of my thigh to the fingers. The three fingers of my right hand – index, middle, and ring – were under temporary plaster as they had been damaged. What I was finding to be most uncomfortable and totally unbearable was something in my mouth. I offered all my resistance to get rid of it. Then Papa, who was standing beside me, took out that thing from my mouth and instead inserted three fingers of his left hand in my mouth saying "OK Son. Now bite as much as you like". I heard that. Now I knew his old fingers were in my mouth. I tried my best not to hurt him. Then I slept again. I don't know for how long. Even today when I record this event on the computer, I can feel his fingers in my mouth and hear his affectionate voice though the event is more than 30 years old and Papa died eighteen years ago in 1984. May God bless his soul.

I remained in this condition for about three days. Then I was better. I remember my room in the private ward, the round-the-clock care by the Hospital employees, and the round-the-clock care especially by my wife Mona, her parents, and other relatives. I shall never have words enough to thank them all.

My wife Mona stayed with me in the private ward of the Mission Hospital for the entire period. She said it plainly that she could not go home alone; she would go home but only with me. I still respect her and her sentiment. I still don't know how to thank her for that. She looked after me and from there only she took treatment for her teeth, which had been badly damaged, and for her left leg which had been almost crushed though there was no fracture.

Most probably on the third day itself , under strict medical care, I walked on my right leg in between the two rails of a wooden structure with my two hands rested on the rails and my left leg a little raised above the ground . Then I walked on my right leg with the help of two crutches under my armpits and my left leg a little raised above the ground. This continued for many days. As I record this story on the computer, after every few minutes, I cannot refrain myself from thanking God for the heavenly blessing - I am alive and all my body parts are normal, healthy and functional.

It had been more than fifteen days in the Hospital and I had started asking when could I go home.. Dr. Shaw said not as long as there was infection in the body or there was any other danger . I asked again after a week and he said that if I was so keen he could give me a LAMA Discharge. I kept quiet more so because one of Mona's two younger brothers, Anuj, had died at the age of 16 years in 1968 due to the lack of proper medical care.

Then after about three weeks i.e. around January 22, I was told that I could go home after a week. I requested Dr. Shaw to let me go on January 27, when we were going to celebrate the Second Happy Birthday of Seema. He agreed but said that first I shall have a new, much lighter and better, plaster on my left leg on January 26. I said OK .Late in the afternoon on January 26 I got a new plaster on my left leg.

Then came the big day. At about 10 in the morning on January 27 I was allowed to go home. Mona sat on the front seat of the Tonga (a horse ridden cart) and I was almost laid on the back seat. We came out of the Hospital first followed on Rikshaw (a man pulled cart with three wheels) by Papa. I saw the sky after a very long time. Was it always that beautiful ? Was the Sun always so flattering on my body? Was the fresh air in the open always so intoxicating? Did the trees always dance? Did the flowers always smile? Was the World always so inviting? Innumerable questions flashed in my mind in no time. I knew their answer. In the past, I had neither found the time nor inculcated the attitude to see and feel these things.

Just as we came out of the main gate of the Hospital on the Station Road, the main road of Bareilly, we saw a UP Government Roadways Bus coming from our right and going to our left i.e. toward the Bus Stand. Actually it was being towed by another Bus. It had been very badly damaged. I told Mona that the Bus was so badly damaged that it appeared to have been bombarded heavily. Mona and I agreed that there was no likelihood whatsoever of the survival of its passengers, if any. We solemnly prayed God for that. We came home.

When we reached home, there were about 50 persons to see and welcome us. Particularly Mona was welcome like Savitri, one of the most respected ladies of Hindu mythology who had taken back the life of her dead husband Satyavan from Yamraj, the God of Death. At home, Papa asked Mona and me if We had seen the damaged Bus while coming out of the Hospital. We said that we had seen it and we also repeated the feelings we had expressed earlier. I saw a faint smile on Papa's lips together with a shadow of deep pain in his eyes. I felt confused. A very intelligent man, he immediately understood me and said in a serious deep voice "This was the Bus in which you all were traveling. Today it has been brought here for repairs after police clearance". Nobody said anything. There was no need . Can there be a more effective mode than silence to express strong feelings ? We all knew that silently we were all thanking God for His unlimited blessings and mercy.

We celebrated Seema's Second Happy Birthday. She was so happy to see all of us at home. So far Sumeet and Seema used to be at home and during the night Seema used to stay with Mona in the Hospital; she was still taking her mother's feed in the night.

Toward the end of February, the plaster was removed. Then started knee mobilization. But the knee would not bend. This was in spite of the twice a day wet heat applied by Mona on my leg ; she did that ignoring her own damaged teeth , crushed leg, and the enormous heat on her soft beautiful hands while applying fomentation. Eventually in the Mission Hospital Bareilly I got admitted again on April 13. Then on April 15 I was given spinal anesthesia again and one of the two steel nails was taken out from below the patella of my left knee . I was told that the other nail and the twisted wire could be taken out later on as and when needed. On April 16 I came home.

Reaching home, I said that I wanted to return to Jodhpur and resume my work. Seema had long ago recovered from the injury on her forehead in a few days. Mona's dental treatment was almost over and her leg was much better. After much discussion, I was allowed. On April 20 myself, Mona, Sumeet and Seema went to Moradabad. There, Suresh and Maya held special prayers for us on April 21. Then On April 22 we proceeded to Delhi, boarded a train and next day on April 23 at noon we reached Jodhpur.

On Jodhpur Railway Station some 40 persons had come to see and receive us including Prof. D. N. Elhance who was not only Chairman of my Department but who was an exceptionally kind and loving man and for whom we still hold reverence in our hearts though he died in January 1985.

We went to 3 / 4B, Polo I our residence in Jodhpur. Oh God, what a relief it was to be back at home after all that had happened. First of all we offered our prayers. Then we gradually resumed the normal life.

But there was more to come. In July I found that the wire in my left patella had started peeping out. I went to the Orthopedics Department of the MGM Hospital Jodhpur. The Doctor said it needed an operation. Within two days, under local anesthesia, the other nail and the twisted wire were taken out. Only then I learnt how the wire had been inserted. Actually the three pieces of the patella had been perforated on the edges and they had been held together with the help of a wire passing through the holes. The wire consisted of two wires put together and twisted together. At about 4 PM, I came home after the operation.

Then my senior colleague Dr. Raj K. Agarwala handed over Seema to Mona and went home; since 9 a.m. he and Mona had been taking care of Seema while Mrs. Ira (the graceful wife of Dr. Agarwala) was looking after Sumeet at her own home. Then my younger colleague Dr. P.R. Ojha also left; he too was with us since 9 AM.

Thus, at last, the final phase of the apparent after-effects of the accident was over.

As any one can see and understand, only the apparent after effects had come to an end. The accident made a permanent impact on our hearts and minds. Since then I have developed many convictions, which I would like to share.

Life is totally uncertain. It can end any moment. We do not know at all if we shall live the next moment. Hence, for every moment of life we should feel grateful to God. We should try to live it in the best possible way and be as happy as possible. We must count our blessings and thank God for them. Not doing that is blasphemy in all the religions of the World. We are ungrateful to God if we ignore what we are blessed with and keep complaining day in and day out about so many trivial things and matters of life. We should never forget the man who complained about not having socks till he saw the man who had no legs. As a result of the accident, for a long time, I could not eat with my right hand or brush my teeth or clean myself or take a shower or sit on the chair or walk or sleep properly or hug my little Seema or play with my little Sumeet or do so many other things of life which we always PRESUME and TAKE FOR GRANTED. One realizes the bliss of these things only when they are absent. Thank God, now I am fine. Ask those people the value of water, for instance, who had to collect rainwater dripping from their housetop, boil it, filter it, and use it due to the water shortage. Or ask those people the value of sunlight that were deprived of it at home during winters for many years and due to which they felt winter cold penetrating inside their bones. Can you guess whom I am talking about ?

Further, if we want to do something good, we should do it without any FURTHER delay because life can end any moment. Since life can end any moment, we should not feel undue attachment with any person or object. We should do our duty always and toward all and we should use and enjoy all objects but it is being less than wise to have undue attachment . Any living or inanimate object can lose its existence in a moment. Such is the truth of life and this World.

It was strangers who helped me in and outside the damaged Bus. It was a stranger – the truck driver – who brought us to Moradabad Hospital. Without the help of these strangers I would have died long ago. So we should be kind and helpful to all others including strangers irrespective of their race, religion, faith, sect, caste, color, profession, social status, and all those considerations which only divide human beings .Lucky are those who get an opportunity to help others and blessed are those normal healthy people who are able to help themselves and do not need anybody else's help.

What happens in our lives depends not only on what we do but also on what others do. And then there is so much which affects us but which is totally beyond our control – we just cannot do anything about it. We have to accept it irrespective of what we call it – Chance, Luck, Destiny or simply God's will. If we are destined to get something – good or bad – we shall get it; we cannot take it if we are not so destined and we cannot escape it if we are destined to get it. Long ago Sheikh Sadi had said – That which is not destined the hand cannot reach and that which is destined shall reach you. Omar Khayyam said the same thing when he wrote "The Moving Finger writes; and, having writ, Moves on : nor all thy Piety nor Wit Shall lure it back to cancel half a line, Nor all thy Tears wash out a Word of it.". That shall always be true.

Smallest actions of the smallest people can lead to greatest disasters. So we should be extremely careful about what we do (including what we think and speak because often it takes only the click of an eye for a thought to be manifested into speech and speech into action). It was only a small mistake of a rural cyclist which inflicted enormous loss and suffering on such a large number of persons. Also, we should not hurt others by our words or actions; who knows whether we shall (or shall not) get another opportunity to do some good in life.

ABOUT THE AUTHOR

Ram Mohan Saxena, Ph.D. (born 1943, Allahabad, India) taught at Lucknow, Jodhpur, and Kumaon universities in India and in Tribhuvan University, Kathmandu, Nepal. Ram also served as an Officer of the Industrial Development Bank of India Bombay and as their Nominee Director.

After resigning from the post of Professor and Head, Department of Commerce, Kumaon University, Nainital, India, Ram is now living in the United States. A believer in family values, he has traveled worldwide.

Long and diverse life experience, coupled with brilliance in writing skill places Ram in a unique position to tell *Grandpa's Stories about India* with maturity, authority, and skill in an entertaining, exciting, and inspirational manner.

Grandpa's Stories about India is Ram's first publication outside the field of professional writings.

Printed in the United States
37252LVS00008B/109